Opal
Dreaming

3
DIAMOND
SPIRIT

Opal Dreaming

KAREN WOOD

ALLEN&UNWIN

First published in 2011

Copyright © Karen Wood 2011

Allen & Unwin
83 Alexander Street
Crows Nest NSW 2065
Australia
Phone: (61 2) 8425 0100
Fax: (61 2) 9906 2218
Email: info@allenandunwin.com
Web: www.allenandunwin.com

Cataloguing-in-Publication details are available from the
National Library of Australia www.trove.nla.gov.au

ISBN 978 1 74237 317 1

Cover photos by James Boulette / iStockphoto;
Hugh Brown / Wildlight
Cover and text design by Ruth Grüner
Set in 11.3 pt Apollo MT by Ruth Grüner
This book was printed in February 2014 at
McPherson's Printing Group,
76 Nelson Street, Maryborough, Victoria, 3465, Australia

5 7 9 10 8 6

1

'*WOOHOO!*' JESS SLID DOWN the front stair rail, her arms out wide, and landed expertly on the driveway. 'Today's the day!'

For the first time in weeks, the sky was a clear blue, and the air was still, not a breath of wind. The sun was warm on Jess's face and everything about the day seemed perfect. She skipped to the feed shed, hauled out some hay and threw it over the fence. 'Come on, Dodger, it's time to go and get Opal!'

Dodger nickered to her and began snuffling at the hay. Jess stepped through the fence and gave the old stock-horse a big hug. 'Eighteen months we've been waiting,' she said, running her hands through his shaggy brown coat. 'I can't *believe* I can finally bring her home!'

She took a brush to him, rubbing in hard circular motions as she talked. 'Opal's a very special filly. She's connected to Diamond. You remember Diamond, don't you?'

As Jess rubbed Dodger's back, the old horse curled his lip with pleasure. She combed out his tail, painted his hooves with grease, and pulled her phone from her pocket to thumb a message.

U guys saddled yet?

Before she could send it, Jess heard a shrill 'Coo-ee!' A clatter of hooves sounded along the road, gradually getting louder. From behind the hedge, she could hear her friends, chatting and laughing.

'I thought you'd have that old stockhorse saddled up by now,' Shara called as she rode through the gate on Rocko.

'Sharsy!' Jess squealed. 'You're home!' The day was becoming more perfect by the minute.

'Dad brought me home for the weekend,' her best friend grinned.

'How's vet school?'

'I'm their star student!'

Rosie followed on her quarter horse. 'You're back on the legend, Jessy!' she said, as she pulled Buster to a halt and jumped off.

Jess gave Dodger a pat on the neck. 'I will be in a

minute.' She picked up her new stock saddle and slung it over his back, pulled the girth through the rig and slapped the fenders down into place.

'Are you excited?' asked Grace, appearing on a leggy chestnut.

'I couldn't sleep last night,' answered Jess, as she reached for her bridle.

'Have you got a little halter for her?' asked Shara.

'We don't need one. We're just going to lead the mare and let Opal follow.'

'What? All the way back to here without a halter?' Shara sounded mildly alarmed.

'Probably the best way. She's never been touched by a human, let alone had a rope on her,' said Jess. She pulled a face. '*Lawson's rules.*'

As part of the purchase agreement with Lawson, Jess had agreed not to handle Opal during her first six months. Lawson didn't like foals being mollycoddled by girls. He said it made them 'rude and disrespectful'.

Shara snorted. 'He's such a killjoy.'

'Not for much longer,' said Jess. 'As soon as she's weaned, she'll be *mine*! I'll have three whole weeks to handle her before she goes out west to Longwood.'

'Wish *we* could go on that trip,' said Grace.

Lawson had inherited a share in his father's grazing property, Blakely Downs, and was taking several horses,

3

including a mob of brumbies, out there for a droving trip. Opal, together with the other young horses, would be turned out onto the station to fatten up on the Mitchell grass. The older horses would be put to work on the stock route, droving fifteen hundred cattle to the saleyards.

'Me too,' Jess sighed. 'Droving would be so much fun.' She rammed a foot into a stirrup and sprang into the saddle.

'Are you leaving Opal's mum with her for a couple of days?' asked Shara.

'Yeah, just overnight to get her settled, then Lawson wants to get Marnie back into work for the droving trip.'

'You'd better look after her,' said Rosie. 'Do you have any idea how much he paid for that mare?'

'Mum reckons it was enough to buy a brand-new car,' said Grace.

'She'll be all right,' said Jess. 'Lawson's been over and checked the fences to make sure she can't hurt herself.'

At that moment a low rumbling noise rolled through the valley, making the ground tremble.

'What was that?' asked Jess, looking up at the cloudless blue sky.

'Storm,' said Grace. 'It's supposed to come through later this afternoon.'

'Look, the sky's turning green over there,' said Shara, pointing beyond the mountains to the south. 'It's gonna be a doozy!'

Jess gathered her reins and kicked Dodger on. 'Let's get going. We don't want to get stuck in it.'

The girls headed towards the river flats. As they followed a well-worn track to the crossing, they could hear thunder rumbling through the valley again.

'That sky's getting darker,' warned Rosie.

'It's coming up over the hills,' said Shara. 'Look!' Behind Mossy Mountain, the sky was turning an eerie mix of green and purple. It suddenly flashed white with the afterglow of distant lightening. 'We're going to get drenched.'

'I don't care – I love riding in the rain,' said Grace.

'So do I, but I hope it doesn't unsettle Opal while we're trying to move her,' said Jess.

Grace scoffed. 'Horses aren't scared of rain.'

'But what if the river rises?' Jess squeezed Dodger into a trot. 'We might not be able to get her through. I couldn't handle having to wait until next weekend to bring her home.'

Dodger swished his tail and gave a skip with a hind leg. He broke into a canter. Jess led the girls down the riverbank and they splashed through the knee-deep water.

Shara cantered up on her shoulder. 'Can't that old gerry go any faster?' she yelled, as she thundered past.

Dodger seized the bit and took off after Rocko, with Buster and Milly following closely behind. Jess gave him the reins and let him stretch his legs. It felt fantastic to be flying along on him again, his hooves making a loud melodic rumble over the grassy flats. She laughed into the wind and kicked him on.

Beyond the grassy flats at the Slaughtering Creek junction, the group reached Katrina Pettilow's place. Her horse Chelpie stood listlessly on a timbered hillside. When the little white mare saw the girls, she pulled a horrible face and charged at the fence.

'Have they weaned Tinkerbell already?' asked Shara, pulling Rocko back to a walk.

'About a month ago,' said Jess. 'Katrina wanted Chelpie back.'

'Did she ever find out about Tinks?'

'Nope. She didn't visit Chelpie once in six months.' Jess shook her head. Her friend Luke had used Chelpie to foster his orphan brumby filly when Chelpie had lost her own foal. The little mare had been a good mother, ferociously protective. 'She's done nothing but pace up and down that fence since Tinks was taken away from her. She looks terrible.'

'Look how skinny she is,' Shara said in disgust.

'Katrina should sell her if she's not interested in her anymore,' said Rosie. 'Poor horse.'

'Chelpie's so sour. Who'd buy her?' said Jess. 'I just wish Katrina would feed her a bit more.'

She looked up at the bank of thick cloud that was swelling behind the mountains – it was moving unbelievably fast – and pushed Dodger into a trot. Chelpie called a screeching whinny as they departed.

The weather caught up with them just as they rode around the bend alongside the old sawmill. Heavy drops speared into their oilskin jackets and rolled down their helmets. Up ahead, Lawson's blue timber house stood as neat as a pin. Perfectly straight fences radiated from brick stables and, in the paddocks, the mango trees were heavy with ripening fruit.

The girls walked the horses through Lawson's fat red cattle dotted about the flats, then rode up the laneway and into the stable block. The rain was deafening on the tin roof, but it was warm and dry inside.

Lawson pulled himself from beneath the horse he was shoeing and stretched. 'I've got another couple of horses to trim before we can move that filly,' he shouted over the din. 'And I've gotta get the cattle in. That river's gonna rise this afternoon.'

Jess's heart sank. Opal was too little to be swimming across rivers, especially fast-flowing ones. 'Do you want *us* to bring them in?' she yelled. 'We can do it while you finish shoeing those horses.'

'Yeah, righto, just don't stir 'em up.'

Shara grinned cheekily. 'Would we do such a thing?'

Lawson frowned. 'You can go down on foot, Shara. Take a bucket of molasses and call them up. Jess, you get behind them on that old stockhorse and do a head count of forty-three.' He raised his voice in the direction of Grace, who was at the other end of the stable block, tethering her horse. 'Gracie, can you slip a halter on that grey out in the yards and bring her in? Leave the big gate open for the cattle to come through.'

Jess rode back out of the building and quickly cast her eyes around the house yard for Luke. She barely saw him now that he was working for Lawson. He was usually out in the work ute, doing the trimming jobs. When he'd worked at Harry's place, she'd always known where to find him, but these days their paths rarely crossed. Jess couldn't see the ute. He must be out again.

She rode down the laneway, Shara clomping behind her. Then, while Shara stood calling out and banging on the bucket, Jess made a wide circle around the cattle. Red and white baldy faces popped out from behind trees, and bellows came from around the bend, as the herd began to wander through the rain towards the molasses. Jess didn't need to do much but sit there and count them as they plodded by. On the other side of the river she thought she could hear Chelpie's distressed whinnying above the sound of the rain.

Jess counted thirty-nine head of cattle, with four

more emerging from the bushes below, and pulled her phone from her pocket to text Shara, who she could see pouring the molasses into the yard trough.

going to check Chelpie, somethgs wrong

She watched Shara pull her phone out, thumb a message and wave to her, as she opened the gate for the cattle.

Buzz, rumble.

Shara: will get Rocko + follow u down.

Jess trotted back across the flats towards the river. The rain pelted at her and she had to keep her chin down to shield her face. As she ducked under tree branches, she could see the white pony in the distance, her hind legs pulling at the fence wire.

Typical. Wish the Pettilows would fix their fences.

As Jess approached, she saw that Chelpie's legs were caught. Jumping down from Dodger, she checked for injuries and found none, so she carefully untwisted the wire and lifted Chelpie's back feet out of the tangled mess. As she slipped off the last of the wire, the mare squealed and lashed out with both hind feet. Jess only just managed to duck, and Chelpie's hooves connected instead with Dodger's flank. Dodger jumped sideways and, finding himself loose, trotted off across the flats with his reins dangling. Chelpie cantered after him.

'Oh, don't run away,' moaned Jess. '*Dod*ger!' She pulled her phone from her pocket and messaged Shara.

can u grab D?

She tucked her phone away and stood waiting, hands on hips. Moments later, Shara emerged from the river on Rocko, leading Dodger behind her. 'What happened?' she asked. 'You okay?'

'It's the last time I help that stupid horse,' said Jess. 'Now we'll have to stuff around for hours trying to catch her.' Her boot squelched with water as she stepped into the stirrup, and a trickle of water crept under her collar and ran down her spine. Her saddle was like a wet sponge.

'She's headed towards Lawson's place,' said Shara, turning Rocko. 'Hope she doesn't make trouble.'

'Great,' mumbled Jess, as she watched Chelpie prancing about in the pouring rain with her tail in the air. 'That's all we need.'

2

WHEN THEY GOT BACK to the stables, Jess took off her helmet and coat and shook her head like a dog, sending sprays of water across the stable. Down the aisle she saw Marnie's head poking out of a stable door.

'Marnie's in the stable!' said Shara, rushing down the aisle. 'Let's see Opal!'

'I brought her in for you, Jessy,' said Grace, hanging a halter on the hook outside her stall. 'Opal just trotted in right behind her.'

Jess ran down the aisle after Shara to the mare's stable. Marnie lifted her nose and sniffed at the girls as they approached. She had the kindest, softest eyes Jess had ever seen on a horse. Jess gave her a pat and peered into the stable at the filly sidling up nervously beside her.

'She's *gorgeous*,' said Shara, leaning an elbow on Jess's shoulder.

Opal peeped out from behind her mother, her long-lashed eyes wide in wonderment at her new surroundings. She had never been inside a building before.

'Hello, little one,' said Jess, beaming. She hadn't seen Opal this close up since the day she was born. She cast her eye over the filly and found her to be every bit as beautiful as she had hoped. She was a rich liver chestnut, glistening gold around her flanks and muzzle, with no white markings except – there they were – the three white diamonds, cascading down her shoulder like falling stars, just like the ones Diamond had had on her hindquarters.

Jess's heart flipped in her chest. 'You're so perfect,' she whispered, running her eyes over the filly's long, elegant neck, straight legs and muscular hindquarters.

'She looks like her daddy, doesn't she?' said Grace from behind them. Grace was very proud of her father's stallion, Muscles.

'They're the same colour. I *love* liver chestnut,' answered Jess.

The stallion's coat changed colour with the seasons. In winter he was dark, almost chocolate brown; after he'd moulted in spring, he turned a brilliant reddish copper. Then, over the hotter parts of summer, he faded to a golden orange. Jess hoped that Opal's coat would do the same.

'What did you decide to call her?' asked Lawson, walking down the stable aisle and joining them at the stable door. He looked over Jess's shoulder at the little chestnut filly.

'Opal,' said Jess, gazing, besotted, at her once-in-a-lifetime horse.

'Bad-luck stones,' grunted Lawson.

'That's total rubbish,' said Jess. 'Can't you ever say anything nice?'

Lawson shrugged. 'She's a well-put-together horse. She'll be an athlete.' He looked at Grace and smirked. 'Gets that from the *mare's* side.'

'Well, she'll have good cattle-sense too, which will definitely come from the *stallion's* side!' Grace poked her tongue out at him.

Lawson cuffed his little cousin on the head. 'Hope she hasn't got the *stallion's* temperament.'

'Muscles is one of the best stallions in the country,' Grace said indignantly. 'There's nothing wrong with his temperament.'

There was a faint buzzing noise above the hammering of the rain and Jess stuck her head out of the stable doorway. It was Elliot Duggin on his minibike.

'Vet deliveries,' said Shara.

Grace ran to the doorway. 'I'll get them. I know where everything goes.'

Elliot reached the stable door and turned around to the back of the bike. He pulled the lid off a large tub that was secured with occy straps. Jess could hear him mumbling something from under his helmet.

'What?' Grace yelled. She knocked on his visor and laughed. 'I can't hear you!'

Elliot pulled off his helmet and blinked at Grace. He always blinked a lot when he wasn't wearing his glasses. 'There's a huge storm on the weather radar. I have to get these deliveries done before it comes over. I did a 3D simulation on the Bureau's Stormwatch game, and it's going to be huge!'

'It already is huge,' said Grace.

'Well, it's going to get huger,' said Elliot.

'How long have we got?'

'A few hours. It just hit Brisbane.' He put his helmet back on, saluted Grace and turned his bike out of the doorway.

'We'd better head off soon,' said Grace, turning to the others. 'Otherwise the river is going to rise and we'll never get through.'

'It's already up to Dodger's knees,' said Jess, looking out the doorway and up at the overflowing gutters. 'It's absolutely belting down!'

'Hey! If the bridge floods over, we won't be able to go

to school!' said Rosie as she walked in from the rain, two empty halters in her hand.

'Oh *derrr*, Rosie. It's Saturday!' said Grace.

'Oh, yeah.' Rosie pulled a tube of lip gloss out of her pocket and uncapped it.

'You must be in love,' said her sister. 'You're going soft in the head over Tom again.'

'You can talk,' said Rosie, running the gloss around her lips and smacking them together. 'You nearly fell over yourself to talk to Elliot.'

'As if,' said Grace, screwing up her nose. 'So, what are you putting *lipstick* on for?'

'I don't know, Grace; what are you such a *feral* for?' her sister retorted.

Lawson led a big chestnut gelding out of a stable. 'Come on, Slinger.' He turned to the girls. 'I'll trim those other horses later. Let's get that filly across the river before the storm hits.'

Relieved, Jess untied Dodger and led him from the stables. A gust of wind pulled at her clothes as she left the shelter of the building.

Lawson rode down the laneway on Slinger, with Marnie behind him on a lead rope, Opal trotting anxiously at her heels. Jess hunched into her jacket and rode after them into the wind and rain.

'Wait for me,' called Shara, vaulting onto Rocko and cantering to catch up. Grace and Rosie rode out of the stables in matching oilskin jackets, and soon the four girls had formed a tightly ridden posse, following Lawson, Marnie and Opal towards the first crossing.

As they rode onto the river flats, Chelpie appeared again. She trotted up behind Opal and wheeled about, tossing her mane and inviting her to play. Jess frowned as she watched the filly turn and trot off behind Chelpie, snorting playfully.

'We should have caught her,' said Shara, as Rocko bumped up beside Dodger. 'She's going to cause trouble.'

'We would have been there all day,' said Jess. 'She's in no mood to be caught – look at her.'

The two horses cantered about the flats, skidding and sliding on the greasy mud, moving further and further from the group.

'She's purposely trying to lead Opal away,' said Shara.

'Marnie will call her back in a minute.' Jess looked hopefully at the mare, who pranced about on the end of her rope, gazing fretfully across the field at Chelpie and Opal. 'It's funny how Chelpie loves foals but she never mixes with other adult horses. She's totally weird.'

'She's spooky,' said Shara.

'Evil,' agreed Jess.

Marnie screamed out to her filly as they reached the

first crossing, and Jess was relieved when Opal came cantering back.

Lawson went through the river first, leading the mare. Instead of following, Opal stood at the top of the bank, looking at the gushing water with curiosity. As she watched her mother splash through, she squealed questioningly. Marnie whinnied back to her.

Opal gingerly put out a hoof and recoiled in fear as water rushed around her leg. She spun and galloped off to the flats with her tail clamped firmly between her hind legs.

'Get out of the way,' said Lawson, waving the girls away from the bank. 'You'll only make her more nervous!'

The girls made room for the filly to come through. Marnie stood in the middle of the river, water swirling about her knees, and let out a shrill cry. Opal trotted back to the edge of the river with noticeably less ping in her stride. She paused on the bank and sniffed at the wild white water. Marnie nickered encouragement.

Everybody stayed still and waited for the filly to make her move. 'Come on, little girl,' whispered Jess. 'You can do it.'

The filly put one, then two unsteady hooves into the rushing river. And there she stood, trembling, snorting and flicking her ears, poised to leap out again at the slightest provocation.

Jess groaned inwardly. This was going to take all day. She moved Dodger away from the river, took a deep breath and tried to mentally arrange herself into a more patient frame of mind, which wasn't easy under the lashing rain.

'Okay, everyone just ride through the river,' said Lawson. 'If we leave her on her own, she should follow.' He was beginning to look annoyed.

'No, no, wait,' said Jess.

'Come on, you lot,' said Lawson to the other riders, ignoring her. 'Let's ride on.'

'But you can't just leave her there!' said Jess, in disbelief.

Lawson turned and rode away. Rosie and Grace shrugged apologetically at Jess and followed him.

Shara looked torn. 'Just *try* riding away, Jess, and see what happens.'

'You go,' said Jess flatly. There was no way she was leaving Opal.

Shara had barely turned Rocko when the filly plunged into the gushing water in a sudden burst of bravery. She landed knee-deep and took a few clumsy steps, bawling pathetically to her mother, before suddenly losing her footing and going belly up. In seconds she was swept downstream with her legs thrashing wildly and her head disappearing under the water.

'Oh God, she's gonna drown,' screamed Jess. 'I *knew* we should have put her on a truck.'

The filly crashed into a fallen log and came to a stop, her two front legs splayed either side of it. She sat there quivering, stricken with terror. Water rushed all around her.

Lawson rode back, breathed something inaudible through his teeth, and glared at the pathetic creature. 'If it had a brain it'd be dangerous,' he seethed at Jess, as though everything was somehow her fault.

'That's not helpful.' Jess was close to tears. 'She's still your horse – don't you even care about her?'

'Thank Christ I sold her,' Lawson muttered.

'Thank Christ, all right,' Jess yelled back.

'Yeah, righto, screeching at me's not gonna solve anything. What are we supposed to do with her now?' Lawson braced his hand on his thigh, surveyed the situation and then answered his own question. 'We'll have to get some ropes and pull her out.'

Jess was horrified. 'She's not even halter broke!'

'Well, what do you want to do with her? Just leave her there to drown?'

'I don't know, but I don't want to go roping her. There must be another way.'

Jess racked her brain for a solution. The trees lining the bank waved madly in the wind, bending and groaning as rain lashed in all directions. Chelpie was still screaming on the flats behind them. This was not how Jess had envisaged bringing home her long-awaited, once-in-a-lifetime filly.

A gigantic bolt of lightning split the sky and the bursting sound of simultaneous thunder nearly turned Jess inside out.

'That was right on top of us!' screamed Shara.

As Jess wheeled Dodger around, a sudden gust of wind blasted her, catching her jacket like a sail and nearly pulling her out of the saddle. There was a wild hissing in her ears and the rain swirled in an eddy, lashing wet strands of hair across her face. Dodger pinned his ears back and reared into the rain.

'Easy, boy,' she yelled.

A twister, white with rain, raced across the flats and smashed itself out into the trees.

'Wild!' Jess shouted to Shara.

'You're not wrong,' yelled Shara, reining a frantic Rocko back under control. As the rain began to pelt down even harder, she called out something else, but the wind snatched away the sound of her voice before it could reach Jess's ears.

Then Grace yelled something equally incoherent and pointed at the water.

Jess squinted at the rain-pelted surface of the river. 'Oh my God, no!' she squealed. A slithery white snake was heading for Opal, borne along by the rushing water.

Jess had seen what a snake could do to a horse. One of Stanley Arnold's geldings had been bitten by a baby snake at a campdraft a year ago and it was still recovering in the paddock. And that was a fully grown horse. Opal was just a pint-sized foal.

In a blink, Lawson dropped the mare's rope and spurred Slinger into the water, his stockwhip drawn. In one swift movement he swung the whip over his head and snapped his elbow back. The cracker cut the surface of the water just as the snake was millimetres from hitting Opal. The sound of it nearly gave Jess a seizure.

Opal exploded out of the water as though a stick of dynamite had detonated under her. She jumped clean over the log and landed head-first in the water on the other side, rolled, scrambled to the edge of the river and pressed her trembling body against her mother's.

'What was *that*?' cried Grace.

'Albino snake,' Lawson shouted against the wind, reining his horse away from the river. 'Dunno what sort it was but I doubt you'd want to hang around and find out.' He rode along the riverbank, collected Marnie's lead rope and pulled her alongside Slinger. A waterlogged Opal followed miserably behind. 'Now, will one of you girls go and catch that ridiculous grey pony before she causes a real accident?'

'It's white,' said Rosie.

'I don't care if it's purple with yellow polka dots, just *catch* the stupid thing!' yelled Lawson.

'We don't have a halter,' said Jess, pushing Dodger up next to him. 'But when we get to the Pettilows' place I'll run in and ask Katrina to grab her.'

'Fine,' said Lawson. 'Now let's get going, or we'll never get these horses moved.'

Jess led the group towards the Pettilows' property, then left them to canter up through a forested easement to the house. The empty carport suggested that no one was home, but Jess called out just in case, lest she be accused of trespassing.

She tied Dodger to a tree and walked cautiously up the front steps onto the verandah, where she spotted a coil of rope by a pile of firewood. She leaned over and grabbed it, then rode back to the flats. 'I found this,' she said.

'Here, hold Marnie, and I'll get a rope around Snow White.' Lawson passed Jess the mare's lead rope, not letting go until he was sure she had a good hold of it. He looked her dead in the eye and said, 'Do *not* let go of my good mare.'

'I've got her,' she assured him.

Lawson fiddled with the rope for a while, tying a loop in one end, then rode over to the wayward horse, who stood with her bony rump to the wind. He slung the rope around her neck and brought her back to Jess. 'Take this pony back to the Pettilows' and put her somewhere dry. See if you can find a rug for her, too – she's got no meat on her bones to keep her warm. She'll get pneumonia. Catch up with us later.' He took Marnie's rope from her and rode off.

Chelpie stood her ground and refused to move.

'Come on,' groaned Jess, pulling at the rope.

The little white mare put her ears back and tossed her head at Jess.

'I'll come with you,' said Shara, riding up behind Chelpie and flicking a rein over her rump. 'Get up, Chelpie.' The little mare lashed out with a hind leg and leapt forward.

Together, Jess and Shara dragged Chelpie back to Katrina's place and found a small stable joined to the shed. Inside, it was full of manure, as though it hadn't been cleaned for weeks. The lower slats of the door were broken and jagged pieces of wood hung from rusty nails.

'She must just stand there chewing on the timber all day,' said Jess, looking at the teeth marks that ran around the entire surrounds of the window. The door latch, she noticed, was smashed.

'It must be where Katrina keeps her so that she stays nice and white,' Shara said in disgust.

Chelpie began to pull away, pinning her ears back.

A waft of rancid urea stung Jess's nose. 'You don't want to go in there, do you?' she said to the mare. 'I don't blame you!'

Chelpie started rearing.

Jess gave the little horse a begrudging pat on the neck. It was the first time she had ever found any warmth in her heart for the horse. 'It's all right, we won't make you go in there.'

'There isn't one other animal here to keep her company, not so much as a chook.' Shara looked around the property. 'What a lonely life.'

'Can you imagine raising a tiny foal in that box all by herself without a mother?' Jess couldn't believe someone would do such a thing just to win a few ribbons.

'No wonder she's a total fruitcake,' said Shara.

Chelpie stopped rearing and stood in the rain, looking miserable.

'I wish I could take her back to Luke,' Jess muttered.

Jess handed Dodger to Shara while she tethered Chelpie in the carport and went looking for some feed. She eventually found a stack of sweet-smelling lucerne bales in a machinery shed, and stared at them in amazement. 'Why doesn't Katrina give any of this to her horse?' she said, as she walked back out with an armful of hay.

The bedraggled white pony began to hoe into it. Meanwhile, Jess found some chaff bags and an old blanket to tie around Chelpie's belly with some baling twine. Jess shook her head. 'Amazing what goes on behind closed doors.'

She jumped up into her saddle and trotted after Shara back to the others. The rain eased for a short moment, and she grinned through the water that dripped from the peak of her helmet. Only another kilometre or so up the river flats, and Opal, her once-in-a-lifetime horse, would be home.

3

JESS LEANED ON the rails of her home yards and smiled defiantly into the rain that beat down on her face. She was completely and utterly saturated but she didn't care. She had her filly home at last, and they had the next three weeks to get to know each other.

Lawson walked up behind her, leading Slinger. Tiny waterfalls ran off the brim of his hat. 'King tide. It's gonna be a big flood.'

In the yard, Dodger, Buster, Rocko and Milly stood tethered, their heads down, rumps turned into the wind and the rain. Marnie and Opal took shelter in the small lean-to. In the paddock beyond, courses of water were forming rapidly flowing rivulets down towards the flats.

'It's lapping at the bottom fences already,' said Jess. 'Lucky we live on a hill. I've never seen it rise so quickly.'

'We won't be able to get these horses out of here

tonight,' said Lawson. 'We might have to leave them here, and pick 'em up when the river goes back down.'

'We've only got one small yard and the grazing paddock.' Jess wished some of her fencing fantasies were already in place. She would love to be able to offer her friends somewhere better to put their horses. 'Rocko will have to go in the yard – he's too vicious to put with the other horses.'

Lawson nodded in agreement. 'Sounds like a good idea.'

Jess's father ran out towards them, his bandy legs bare below a hooded raincoat. 'Put them out in the paddock, Lawson. I'll get some hay for them.'

'Thanks, Craig,' said Lawson, He led Slinger to the paddock gate.

Craig joined Jess at the yards. 'Happy now you got your baby home?' He put an arm around her shoulder and gave her a squeeze, causing a new trickle of water to run down her back, making her shiver.

'Isn't she beautiful, Dad?' she said, smiling at him. 'See the three markings on her shoulder? Just like Diamond's.'

They watched as Lawson opened the yard gates and let the mare and foal out into the big paddock. Marnie ran her nose along the ground and snorted at all the moving water. Opal tottered nervously behind.

Jess turned to go inside. There was always a sense of

excitement when the river flooded. People got holed up and life was put on pause for a day or two. Part of her was glad that Rosie, Grace and Shara were all trapped at her place by the floodwaters. They could have a sleepover.

As she sloshed her way back to the house, she remembered Chelpie. 'Don't let me forget to ring Katrina, Dad. We caught her horse running feral down on the flats. She's tied up in their carport.'

'What, *again*?'

'Katrina's too busy chasing boys to look after her horse these days.'

'Well, when *you* start running after boys, I hope you will still look after Opal properly.'

Jess slung her halter playfully at him. 'I would never run off after a boy and forget my horse.'

'Oh yeah, that's what you say now,' he teased. 'But don't worry; your mother and I will look after Dodger in his old age when Mr Spunky-pants comes along.'

'I promise you, Dad, if I ever run away from my horses, it won't be with someone called *Mr Spunky-pants*.'

'Come on,' Craig chuckled, 'you'd better look after your visitors.'

Jess found Shara, Grace and Rosie taking shelter under the house. They had dumped their saddles in a big pile near the back stairs. 'Dad said you can all stay overnight.'

'Hey?' said Craig from behind her. 'How come I don't remember saying that?'

'You said I'd better look after my visitors,' Jess shrugged. 'It's the same thing.'

'Great!' said Shara. 'Where will we put the horses?'

All three girls began to text their parents.

'I'm going to drop Lawson home while I can still get the car through the floodwaters,' Craig said. 'Get those horses turned out and then go inside and dry off, hey?' He turned and headed for the ute.

As Lawson hopped into the passenger seat, he said, 'Look after that mare for me, Jess. She's going droving in a few weeks.' He sounded uncharacteristically jolly.

'I will!' she smiled.

Lawson looked over into the paddock at the mare and foal. 'Bring Opal over to Harry's place once she's weaned and we can put her in with Luke's foals. They can buddy up before we let them go on the station together.'

Jess gave a reluctant nod. She didn't want to start planning Opal's departure yet – she'd only just got here. Three weeks seemed like such a tiny amount of time to handle and get to know her. But Jess knew Blakely Downs would be a fantastic start in life for Opal, running free in a big mob on good-quality pasture, and she tried to remind herself that they'd have the rest of their lives to be friends.

When the horses were turned out and fed, her friends piled into the bathroom to get showered off. Jess made a phone call while she waited her turn.

'Hello, Mrs Pettilow? This is Jess Fairley.'

After a short pause, a cold voice answered her. 'Yes, Jessica?'

'I was riding past your place today and Chelpie got out. She was galloping around the—'

'Oh, she got out, did she?' Mrs Pettilow interrupted. 'Sure you didn't *let* her out?'

'Pardon?'

'Someone saw you handling our horse by the fence, Jessica, so don't bother ringing up with a pack of lies about her getting out,' said Mrs Pettilow. 'Ever since you lost that pony of yours in the cattle grid, you've been trying to blame Chelpie. You tried to lure her down to that same grid with that young filly today, didn't you? Of all the cruel things to do, to take it out on an innocent animal.'

'Cruel?' Jess couldn't believe her ears. 'Chelpie nearly got my foal killed. Did your neighbour tell you that bit?'

'See!' said Mrs Pettilow. 'Here you go blaming Chelpie for your own carelessness again. You had a young horse with no halter on, running around the river flats and now that something's gone wrong, you're looking for someone else to blame.'

'But—'

'Chelpie is an extremely valuable horse; we hand-raised her from when she was a tiny foal and if anything's happened to her, I'll be sending you the vet bill. You need to be a lot more responsible with your horses, Jessica Fairley!'

Jess listened open-mouthed to the mad monologue on the other end of the line. Valuable? Why didn't the Pettilows look after Chelpie better if she was so valuable? She remembered now why she couldn't stand anyone in that family. 'No, Mrs Pettilow. That's not what happened. If you would just listen to me—'

The phone line went dead. Jess pulled the receiver away from her ear and glared at it before slamming it back into its cradle.

She returned to the kitchen. 'I can't believe it – she just hung up on me!'

'Who – Mrs Pettilow?' asked Grace, walking out to the hallway in Jess's favourite red pyjamas. 'Why? What did she say?' Grace liked to know everything that went on in the gully, especially if it involved the Pettilows. She was their number-one critic.

'She accused me of luring Chelpie out to the flats on purpose – so she would get caught in the cattle grid.'

'You're kidding!' snorted Grace.

'Just shows the way they think,' said Rosie, appearing

in Jess's old chenille bathrobe, a scrunched-up bundle of flannelette in her hand. 'Do you have any pyjamas that are a bit more . . . feminine?'

'She said I was cruel!' said Jess, too outraged to answer her.

Shara stepped out of Jess's room in her daggiest old tracksuit and let out a long, loud raspberry. 'Their horse is so skinny it's nearly a welfare case. You should see the state of its stable!'

'Just anything that doesn't resemble a sweaty old work shirt,' said Rosie, holding the offending item between a thumb and forefinger. 'Cotton would be good. I don't do synthetics.'

In the kitchen, the new oven timer beeped incessantly. 'Festy fat fibber. I hate her,' Grace announced as she came face to face with Jess's mum. 'Hello, Mrs Fairley. I think your stove's about to reverse over someone.'

'Hate is such a strong word, Grace,' said Caroline, pushing randomly at buttons, trying to switch the thing off. It finally silenced and she pulled a dish from the oven, releasing delicious-smelling wafts of butter pastry.

'You'll hate her too when you hear what she said to Jess,' said Grace.

'To hate is to give away your power,' said Caroline. 'Who are you talking about?'

The girls all answered at once, filling Caroline in on the day's events, and relaying the Pettilow accusations in peeved tones. They devoured the free-range chicken and leek pie, then systematically emptied every biscuit barrel in the house, washing it all down with Milo as they went.

'You kids are like a plague of locusts,' Caroline complained as she wiped up after them.

The girls emptied the linen closet of blankets and doonas, moved the furniture and set up camp around the open fireplace in the lounge room. When night fell, they turned off the lights and pretended they were sitting around a drover's campfire, toasting marshmallows until they were burnt and crunchy on the outside and gooey in the middle.

'Why are boys always allowed to do fun things like droving?' said Grace. 'Luke and Ryan get to go to Longwood. Dad's going, even Tom.'

'It'll be such an easy run,' agreed Rosie. 'There'll be no bulls. I don't understand why we can't go.'

Grace scowled. 'It's always the same. The men in this family are total chauvinists.'

'I thought Lawson hated Ryan,' said Jess.

'Not so much since he stopped drinking,' said Rosie, always a good source of gossip. 'It was Harry's dying wish that they make up and get along. Lawson's giving him one chance. They're going to take the last of Harry's cattle to the saleyards together, kind of like a tribute to him.' She rolled her eyes. 'That's if they can do it without killing each other.'

'Yeah, and meanwhile, all the *girls* in the family get left behind,' complained Grace.

After more grumbling, Shara began to tell stories of mythical river creatures, bunyips and cursed white snakes, lurking in the riverbeds and waterholes of Coachwood Crossing. When Jess finally fell asleep, her dreams brimmed with images of Chelpie, a skeletal white ghost horse, splashing through swampy river flats, hunting for prey.

4

JESS STAGGERED AROUND in a white haze. The wind tore at her skin, infusing her with an icy coldness, and whipping her hair across her face. Hoof beats clattered in her head, getting louder and louder, circling her. A skeleton with three hollow eyes galloped out of the haze, screaming. Jess screamed back.

'Holy—!' Shara sat bolt upright. 'You scared the bejingles out of me, Jess! What's wrong?'

Jess put both hands on her heart. 'I had a nightmare,' she panted. 'I can still hear it.' She stared wildly about her as though a horse might burst through the walls at any moment. 'Hoofbeats.'

Shara rushed to the window. 'It's the horses. They're going crazy!'

Jess and Grace threw their quilts off and joined her. They couldn't see a thing in the darkness but they could hear galloping hooves and, far away, a horse screaming.

'Something's wrong!' said Jess.

They rushed out to the hallway and pulled on their jackets. Jess grabbed a torch from the hall cupboard. Halfway down the steps she stopped. 'Do you think we should wake Rosie?'

'She'll spit if we go without her,' said Shara.

'She doesn't like having her beauty sleep interrupted,' warned Grace.

'She'd want us to wake her, surely,' said Jess.

Grace groaned and they raced back inside.

'Oi, Noddy!' Grace threw a balled sock at her sister's head.

'Don't,' Rosie whined, pulling her doona around her.

Shara gave Rosie a gentle shake. 'The horses are going off! Wake up, Rosie!'

A grumbling squeal came from Rosie's pillow and an arm swiped at Shara's hand.

'See, told you. You're wasting your time,' said Grace.

'Forget it. Let's just go,' said Jess.

Outside it was pitch black. They heard Rocko scream excitedly to the other horses from the confines of the yard and, from somewhere in the darkness, a hysterical whinny echoed back.

'That's Marnie!' said Jess. 'Opal must be in trouble!'

Jess led the girls fumble-footed into the night, guided only by a small streak of torchlight and the sound of hooves. The air was thick with drizzle, so fine that she could feel it drawn into her lungs as she panted ahead of her friends. They reached the paddock fence.

'I can't see a *thing*,' Grace whined, clutching Jess's arm.

'There's a track a bit further ahead.' Jess climbed over the rail and pushed on. She brandished the torch around, straining her eyes to see the horses. They were close, she could hear them. She found the track and broke into a slow jog.

She led her friends down a steep rocky hill and when they reached the bottom, Jess shone the torch around. Beyond them was a lake of water with just the top few inches of fenceposts jutting from the surface.

Holy . . .

'The river is nearly over the fenceposts,' gasped Jess. 'If the horses go in there, they'll get their legs tangled in the wires.' She ran towards the sound of hooves. '*Where's Opal?*' She shone the torch up and down the fenceline, anxiously searching, as a big black shadow whinnied loudly and galloped along the water's edge. 'Marnie,' cried Jess. 'Where's your baby?'

'Shine it out further, past the fence,' said Shara. 'Opal might be stuck on the other side.'

Jess shone it out further but the light faded into black distance.

'*There!* What was that?' said Shara. 'Shine it back the other way.'

Jess did so and she could just make out a flash of white with two glowing embers on the other side of the river. Two haunted eyes stared at them.

'It's Chelpie! She's escaped again,' Jess groaned. 'Oh God, this can't be happening. *Where is Opal?*'

'Just stop and be quiet for a minute. We might hear her,' said Shara.

Jess stood stock-still and listened, but all she could hear was her own breathing. Then there was a splash. 'What was that?'

'Give me the torch, Jess,' said Shara, taking it from Jess and shining it to the left. 'Come on! She's down here. I can hear her.' She ran in the direction of the splashing.

'That's her!' Jess screamed in a panic. 'Chelpie must have called her to the fence!' She began wading into the water. 'I'm coming, Opal. I'm coming.'

'Don't go out there, Jess,' screamed Grace. 'The current is too strong.' Her voice became hysterical. 'It's a king tide. You'll drown!'

'Get out of there, Jess,' Shara yelled.

The water felt like a moving wall. It bulldozed Jess's legs out from under her and she fell backwards with a splash. She reached frantically down to the soil and grabbed hold of a clump of grass, pulling herself back out. 'Opal's tangled in the fence. Her head keeps going under.'

'I know, but you'll get swept away if you go in after her,' said Shara, clutching Jess by the sleeve.

'But I can't just stand here and watch her drown.' Jess paced up and down, frantic. She could just make out her filly struggling in the fence, her ears flat back and forelegs paddling at the water eddying and roiling around her.

'We need wirecutters. I'll jump on Buster and get some from the shed.' Shara sprang onto Rosie's horse like a jockey and began galloping back to the house.

It seemed like an eternity before Shara returned. Jess stood on the edge of the water in the blackness, running her hands anxiously through her wet hair and pacing while Opal splashed about.

'Don't give up, Opal,' called Jess. 'Don't give up, we're going to help you, just don't give up . . .'

Then she saw two red eyes bobbing along the top of the water.

'Go away, Chelpie!' Jess screamed. She stood up and waved her arms at the horse. '*You* did this.'

'Look,' said Grace, 'I think she's trying to help her.'

Chelpie reached the fence and put her nose under the filly's neck, helping her to stay upright.

Jess watched in amazement. 'That's what we need to do,' she said with a sudden surge of hope, 'get on the horses. They're strong enough to stand in the moving water.' She turned and began to run back into the paddock. 'Dodger, come on. Come on, boy.'

She heard his familiar deep nickering as he came lumbering out of the darkness. Jess wrapped her coat around his neck and jumped onto his back. As she steered him with her legs down into the rushing water, a large beam of light swung through the paddock.

'It's your dad. He's brought the fourbie down,' said Grace excitedly. The four-wheel drive rumbled towards them, pulled up, and Craig, Caroline and Shara all climbed out.

'Don't you even *think* of riding into that water, Jessica Fairley!' Craig ordered. 'You'll be swept away forever.'

The headlights shone directly at the two horses in the swollen river. Only their heads were above the surface, and the water swirled madly around them, leaving a trail of bubbles that raced off downstream. Opal looked utterly exhausted; her head hung over Chelpie's brilliant white neck with a dull expression. Chelpie also looked like she was struggling and her pleading hollow eyes squinted into the headlights.

'Did you bring the wirecutters, Dad?'

'Yep, and some ropes. We'll have to get a halter on that filly somehow.'

'Her legs are stuck in the wire. I'll ride Dodger out there. He's strong enough to take me through the water.'

'It'll just grab you by the legs and rip you straight off him,' said Craig.

Caroline agreed. 'I don't want you in those floodwaters, Jess. Get off that horse now.'

'But there's not much time, they can't stand up for much longer! Someone has to help her!'

'Well, it's not going to be you. Get off that horse, Jess!' yelled Caroline.

'I'll tie a rope around my waist and swim out,' said Craig.

He fastened one end of a rope to the bullbar of the car, then he made a loop with the other end and tossed it out to the nearest fencepost. It missed. Jess ran into the water to help him drag it back in.

'Get *out* of the water,' Caroline yelled.

Jess stepped only halfway out, and shifted from one foot to another as she watched Craig throw it out again. After several attempts, he managed to secure it, then slung another coil of rope over his shoulder, bit the cutters between his teeth and waded in.

An unbearable pain tightened in Jess's throat as she watched her father move closer to the horses. It was slow going, and he was buffeted by the tide at every step.

'Be *careful*, Craig,' Caroline called out. 'Don't let go of that rope!'

When he reached Opal and Chelpie, he slipped a loop around the filly's neck, tied it off and then did the same for the white mare. He took the wirecutters and began to fumble around under the water.

'He's got the rope over her neck. She's going to be okay, Jess,' said Shara. 'We've just got to pull her out now.'

Jess couldn't speak. She stood watching, her hands over her mouth, until her father made his way back to them, then ran in up to her knees to help him out of the water.

'I've cut the wire, but there are still bits of it tangled around her legs,' he panted. 'I couldn't get very close to her feet, she was kicking too much.'

'Dodger can pull them out and we'll get the wire off them later,' Jess said, taking the rope from him. 'Are you okay?'

Craig nodded, still breathless. 'Get Dodger.'

Jess brought Dodger over by a hank of his mane and turned him with his tail to the water. Craig helped her to tie the rope around his neck. Then, taking him by the mane, Jess urged Dodger to pull.

He picked up the slack, then came to a halt as he felt the weight against his shoulders.

'It's okay, Dodger. You have to pull,' said Jess, tugging at his mane. The old horse stepped into the weight and stopped again.

Craig moved back to his rump and put a hand around his tail, giving him a push and making clicking noises. 'Come on, old fella!'

Dodger took a few more steps, his feet slipping in the mud.

'That's it, Dodger, that's it,' said Jess. He kept pulling and she looked back to see Chelpie moving towards them through the water. The filly's head began to slip off her neck. 'Pull, Dodger, pull,' she yelled. She jumped up onto his back and kicked him in the ribs. 'Pull, Dodger,' she yelled. '*Pull!*'

Dodger strained at the rope, with everyone calling encouragement, until Chelpie's bony white body emerged from the river. She trudged through the last few shallow metres with Opal dragging limply beside her.

Craig pulled a knife from his pocket and cut the rope from both horses. Marnie appeared from the dark paddock, screamed loudly and rushed at Chelpie. The white horse snorted and disappeared into the blackness.

Meanwhile, Opal lay with her head on the ground, making horrid gurgling noises. With a splutter, she cleared her lungs. Two strands of wire were still twisted cruelly around her hind legs.

43

'Stand back and let her mum smell her,' said Jess, leading Marnie to her foal.

Opal made tiny moaning noises while her mother nuzzled her.

Jess looked at her filly in despair. 'I'll try to hold her head while you cut the wire, Dad,' she said. 'Shara, can you keep Marnie nearby to help her stay calm?'

The next ten minutes were awful. Jess lay across the filly's neck and sobbed while Craig tried to cut through the wire without hurting her. But when he had finished, his hands were sticky with blood.

'How badly is she hurt?' Jess asked her father.

'It's hard to tell,' said Craig. 'We'll have to get her up to the shed and hose her legs off so we can look at them properly. She'll need a vet to look at her in the morning. That's if he can get through the floodwaters.'

He opened the hatch at the back of the four-wheel drive and they all strained to heave the filly into the back. Jess sat at her head while Shara sat on the tailgate and led the mare behind them.

Under proper lighting in the shed, Craig hosed off Opal's legs and found several deep wounds that needed stitching, but all they could do was slosh some salt water over them and keep them clean. They broke open bales of straw and made a makeshift stable. Opal lay limply, her head outstretched.

Jess sat on the haystack staring at her.

'There's nothing more you can do, honey,' said Caroline gently. 'Come back up to the house and come to bed. You'll be more use to her in the morning if you've had some sleep.'

'I can't leave her, Mum.'

'Her mother is there with her. She'll be more relaxed without people around her.'

'I promised I'd ring Lawson if anything happened. He's going to freak.'

'It wasn't anyone's fault. He won't be angry. Anyway, Marnie is fine. It's the filly that got hurt.'

'Do you think I should ring him now?'

Caroline looked at her watch. 'It will be daylight in a couple of hours. You can ring him then. No point everyone losing sleep.'

While the rest of the house fell back to quietness, Jess sat peering out the lounge-room window. A thin stream of light shone from the shed. She pictured Opal lying listlessly in the straw, her legs torn and her lungs full of muddy water. 'Surely I'm not going to lose another one,' she whispered to herself. 'That would just be too unfair.'

5

THREE DAYS LATER, Jess stood with John Duggin, Shara and Craig outside the yard. Only now had the floodwaters gone down enough for the vet to be able to get through. It was the worst flood the gully had seen for a decade.

John had given Jess instructions over the phone, but every time she tried to get near Opal's legs to clean the wounds, the filly bared her teeth and charged at her. She hadn't eaten and her flanks were sucked in against her hips, leaving caverns of hunger down each side. Now she stood in the makeshift stable with her nose screwed into a permanent scowl and her head cocked awkwardly to one side.

John stood with his legs apart, arms folded, and a serious look on his face while the girls waited eagerly for his diagnosis. 'The leg's not too bad. It probably should've been stitched, but we should be able to get that right with some antibiotics and a bit of iodine.' He paused. 'I'm more worried about that head injury.'

'Head injury?' said Shara, who had delayed going back to boarding school to support Jess and to learn as much as possible from John.

'See the way she's holding her head to the side?' John tilted his own head as he studied the filly. 'That's not right.'

'I thought she was doing that because of the pain,' said Jess.

'It's pain, but it's from her head, not from her leg. Did you say you dragged her out with a rope?'

'Yes.'

'Around her neck?'

'It was the only way,' said Jess. 'She would have drowned otherwise.'

'With another horse right near her, you say? Could she have been kicked in the head, do you think?'

'Yes, easily,' said Jess. 'She was thrashing around and kept going under the water.'

'Could it be an ear infection?' Shara asked.

'It could be,' John replied, 'but I really need to examine her properly to be sure.'

'I can't get anywhere near her,' said Jess. 'She's never been handled before.'

John looked thoughtful. 'We might have to get her

onto a truck and bring her down to the surgery. I'm sorry, but she's a real mess and she's going to need a lot of care for a couple of weeks. I don't think you'll be able to manage her on your own if she's not halter broke.'

'We'll have to take the mare too, then, won't we?' Jess said.

'It would probably be a good idea.'

Jess groaned. 'Lawson's going to freak. He wants to take Marnie droving next week. We'd planned to be weaning Opal now.'

'It seems a bit cruel to wean her while she's so sick,' said John. 'Opal really doesn't need any added stress at the moment.'

Craig stepped in. 'I'll give Lawson a ring and ask if he minds letting the mare go with Opal, at least for a few days. He might lend us his truck too.' He set off towards the house.

Jess slumped against the wall, feeling totally deflated. She had been busting to show John Duggin her new filly, but not like this.

John gave her arm a gentle rub. 'She's going to be fine, Jess. There's no way we'll lose this one, promise.'

'Thanks, John,' she said. 'You don't know how much I needed to hear that!' She used her shirt to wipe away the tears. John was the best vet in the whole world. If he promised that Opal would get better, she believed him.

He had never promised her that with Diamond.

'Where's the other horse you wanted me to see?'

'Over in the yards,' said Jess, leading him to where Chelpie stood looking lethargic and hungry. 'You know Katrina Pettilow's horse, Chelpie?'

As John walked around the shed to the yards he stopped in his tracks. 'Is that her?' His face didn't give a lot away, but Jess knew that anyone who had seen this horse in her glory days would be utterly shocked at her appearance now. 'How did she get here?' he asked.

'She keeps breaking out of her stable and escaping to the river flats. It's because she's so hungry, I reckon.'

'Katrina locks her up and forgets to feed her,' added Shara. 'She's been here since the night of the flood.'

John stepped through the lower rails of the yards and walked up to Chelpie with a hand out. She screwed up her nose at him, then resumed staring into space. The vet raised a hand to her neck and ran it over her shoulder. Muttering something under his breath that Jess didn't catch, John moved to her head. He pulled her eyelids down and inspected them, and opened her mouth to press at her gums.

'She looks pretty bad, don't you think?'

John looked Chelpie all over, then nodded. 'Yeah, she's not a happy horse.'

Craig came back down from the house. 'Lawson said

we can go to his place and pick up the truck now. He's just finishing off a job, then he's going to come over and check on the mare.'

'That's settled then,' said John. 'I'll see you at the surgery in a couple of hours.'

'What about Chelpie?' asked Jess.

'I'll make some phone calls,' said John.

At the clinic, the filly was heavily sedated and settled in a large stable. It had taken both Craig and John to restrain her. She still thrashed about so wildly that John gave her a needle to knock her out, saving them all from trauma and bruises.

John let Jess and Shara assist as he tended to Opal's leg wounds and injected a cocktail of drugs into a dripline, then squeezed and poked and pulled at her head. He looked into her mouth and put his gloved fingers into her ears. 'I can't find anything obvious. With any luck it's just an ear infection from the floodwater and the antibiotics will fix it.' He removed the drip and face cover. 'She'll wake up in half an hour or so.'

While Shara followed John up the stable aisle, pestering him with questions about antibiotics and anaesthetics, Jess sat beside the unconscious foal and stroked her neck gently. As she ran her hand over Opal's thick, soft foal fur, she realised that it was the first time she had ever patted her. She ran her hand between the filly's ears and rubbed her forehead. 'You're going to be okay, little sweetie,' she whispered. 'You're my once-in-a-lifetime horse, and I'm going to look after you no matter what, okay?'

Jess ran her hand over Opal's shoulder and traced her fingers slowly around the three white markings, just like she used to do with Diamond. 'We're going to be the best of buddies, Opal.'

Lawson agreed to leave Marnie there for a few days to keep the foal settled, but he was firm that the mare would then be going droving. The six-week trip had been organised for months and he'd be needing his good horse if he was to go. Jess knew there was no way Lawson would miss out on this trip for the sake of a scrawny, chance-bred foal. It was his way of saying goodbye to Harry. Ryan had already headed off and was organising permits and camping gear, but Lawson and Luke needed to finish up work with several of their clients before they left.

As Jess and Shara jumped up into Lawson's truck to leave the vet's, another car pulled into the surgery carpark. It towed a white float with the letters RSPCA on the side of it. In the back of the float, Jess could make out the knobbly spine of a white horse. She gasped. 'It's Chelpie!'

'Oh my God, Katrina's going to *spew!*' Shara stared at Jess, scandalised.

'Get ready for some nasty phone calls,' said Craig.

Jess chuckled. 'We're going to need a new private number!' She strained around in her seat and looked out the window. A woman was opening the front door to the float. She quickly jumped back as a white nose lunged at her, baring an angry set of teeth.

'Yep, that's Chelpie, all right,' said Shara.

'Wow, Chelpie taken by the RSPCA . . .' Jess could hardly believe it.

'Talk about falling from grace,' said Craig.

After school the next day, Jess visited Opal at the vet's, and was annoyed to find that Chelpie occupied the stall next door to her filly's. Chelpie was alternating between biting and chewing on the timber door and rocking from side to side with her head between her legs.

'She's a basket case,' said Jess, peering over the stable door at the wretched white horse.

'I've never had one so bad,' said John, joining her.

'She's been stabled since she was a week old. No herd to run with.' He shook his head. 'Totally dysfunctional.'

'Does she have to be next door to my horse?' asked Jess.

'It's the only other horse she likes,' said John, apologetically. 'She won't eat unless she's next to Opal.'

'Wouldn't she be happier in a paddock?'

'Undoubtedly,' said John. 'She just needs a few days to pick up and then we'll try to integrate her into a herd, if we can find one.'

Jess moved on to Opal's stall. The filly rushed to hide behind her mother as soon as Jess opened the stable door, where she stood with her ears back and a hind leg raised. She was jittery and nervous, impossible to catch, and John had to sedate her again to handle her. Jess tried to help John while he updated her needles and checked her over. It did seem that Opal was looking healthier. Her temperament, however, was a different story.

As the filly grew stronger she became more difficult to handle. The following day, John was able to catch and restrain her, jostling her to the ground. Jess had to hold Opal down by the neck while the vet checked her temperature and injected antibiotics and other drugs. But the whole forceful episode just made Jess wish he had sedated her again.

On the third day, the filly rushed at Jess as she

approached the stable, slamming hard against the stable door. Jess backed away, hurt and distressed, and waited for John to come and help. When she did manage to get a look over the stable door, she noticed that Opal's head stayed slightly tilted, and one ear seemed to lop unevenly to one side. As John finished another round of X-rays, Lawson arrived with a horse float to pick up Marnie.

'You promised you would leave her here until Opal was better,' said Jess, as he walked towards the stable with a halter in his hand.

'I promised I'd leave her for a few days, Jess,' Lawson corrected her. 'And *you* promised *me* I could bring her back into work after seven months. It's already been ten. Sorry, but I need my good mare back.' He looked through the stable door just as Opal rose groggily to her feet. As John put a hand out to help her, she reared away from him, shaking her head violently and stumbling backwards.

Lawson watched the filly pull itself up off the ground, his face grave. 'Are you sure all this is worth it?'

'What do you mean?' asked Jess.

'I mean, look at her,' said Lawson. 'She's got her father's temperament. She'll be totally unpredictable. Why do you think I'm selling her to you so cheap?'

'She's just sick, that's all,' said Jess.

At that moment, Opal lunged at John. 'Whoa!' he said, waving her away.

54

'Sick horses don't do that,' said Lawson, opening the stable door and walking in. He raised an arm at Opal and yelled, *'Get out of it!'*

Then he haltered Marnie, led her out of the stable and looked Jess in the eye. 'There are a lot of other good fillies out there, Jess. I can help you find one if you like. You don't need to pay me for this one.'

Jess looked at him, bewildered. 'What are you saying?'

'I'm just saying it might be kinder to . . . find something else.'

'No way!' said Jess. 'How could you even think that?' She looked around for John, who was letting himself out of the stable.

'I don't think we need to consider that yet,' said John, frowning at Lawson.

'Go away,' said Jess, angrily. 'Take Marnie and just go home, Lawson. I'll drop your money off later this afternoon.'

Lawson tried a gentler tone. 'If you want my opinion—'

'I *don't* want your opinion,' said Jess, her voice rising. 'I already *know* what your opinion is!'

'No, you don't, so shut up and listen,' snapped Lawson.

Jess set her jaw hard, folded her arms tightly across her chest and glared at him.

'If you really want her to get better,' Lawson began, 'then we should wean her as soon as possible. Don't leave it until she's on a truck and on a long stressful journey to Longwood. Give her a couple of weeks at Harry's place to bond with the other young horses, and then let me take her out to the station. You should still put her out there and see if she heals. Do or die. If she's got any heart, if she's worth her salt at all, then she'll fight. She'll get through it.'

Jess looked to John, who stood listening with his hands in his pockets. He nodded at her. 'I think Lawson could be right, Jess. She's obviously had some sort of knock around the head, but there's nothing showing in her X-rays. I've treated her with some long-acting antibiotics and pretty much done all I can for her. It's up to her now. She needs to go and heal.'

Jess looked at Opal, pacing anxiously around the stable, occasionally stumbling with the lingering effects of the sedatives. She would be a mess when they totally wore off. But she looked generally upright and alive – there was no way Jess was giving up on her yet.

'Can you leave Marnie here for just one more night? Please?'

He dropped his shoulders and let out a slow, unimpressed sigh.

'Come *on*, Lawson,' she begged. 'Just one more night

and I promise I won't argue anymore. Tomorrow Marnie and Opal can travel together to Harry's place and I'll put her in with Luke's brumbies. Then you can take Marnie home.'

She also wanted to get Opal away from Chelpie. She had a gnawing feeling that the filly would come good if Jess could just get her away from that psycho white horse. She looked pleadingly at Lawson.

Lawson gave a reluctant nod. '*One* more night, then.'

6

JESS STUCK TO her word and helped wean Opal the next day at Harry's place. They put the filly in with Luke's two brumby foals, Rusty and Tinkerbell, and Jess spent the afternoon listening to her scream piteously for her mother while she paced about the yard.

Over the next week the filly gradually stopped pacing, and stood sour-faced in a corner by herself.

As Jess stood by the yard gate, Luke walked out of the stables with a bucket of tools in one hand. He seemed even lankier than when she last saw him, and his rusty brown hair was as wild as ever. He still lived at Harry's, helping Annie to take care of the place in return for his keep. Lawson had helped him convert a couple of the stables into a flat.

'How's she going?' he asked, as he joined her at the gate.

'Anytime I try to go in there she just rushes at me,' said Jess. 'I can't get anywhere near her.'

'Don't forget she's only just been weaned. She's had a rough week,' said Luke.

'I wish she'd eat a bit more. She's so skinny.' Jess watched Opal cower behind the other horses in the yard. She had tried to tempt the filly with everything from bran mashes steeped in molasses to small portions of oats. Opal remained uninterested.

'She'll put weight back on when she goes out onto the station and settles in a bit more.'

But Jess knew it was more than just weaning. Something was wrong. It wasn't Opal's body that was sick. It was her spirit. 'I don't want her to go,' she said, 'not while she's so . . . miserable.'

'She's not happy, that's for sure,' Luke said, pulling out his chaps. He swung them around his waist and began to buckle them over his jeans. 'Do you want me to give Dodger a trim?'

'Sure, that'd be great.' Jess opened a stable door and pulled Dodger out. In the next stable, Luke's two wolf-dogs whimpered and barked. Filth stuck his wet nose between a gap in the doors and Fang howled. With their huge feet and soft, shaggy coats, they were like bears, the most huggable of dogs. 'Can I let them out for a run?'

'Yeah,' Luke shrugged.

Jess unlatched the door. She threw a stick for Filth and Fang and laughed as they gambolled clumsily after it. She swung Dodger around and stood him up for Luke. 'Thanks for doing him on your day off.'

'No biggy,' said Luke, reaching for a hoof.

Jess sat on an upturned bucket and let Dodger put his big head in her lap. She scratched his forehead while she watched Luke work.

Luke reached a hand out behind him. 'Pass me the trimmers?'

She peered into his toolbox and rummaged around. 'These ones?'

'Yep.' Luke grabbed them and got to work on the hoof.

'Lawson reckons Opal's got a bad temperament,' said Jess. She grabbed a rasp and held it out, anticipating his next request.

'Ta.' Luke reached back and took it from her hand.

'But it's just all this forceful handling she's had,' said Jess. 'It's teaching her to hate people.'

'She'll be okay with the right handling. Harry always said, "The younger they are, the more you can turn them around."'

'Wish Harry was here now so he could tell me what to do,' Jess said, almost to herself.

Luke spoke from under Dodger's belly, still cheerful.

'Yeah, he would've known what to do with her.' He finished the front hoof, dropped it, ran a hand over Dodger's hindquarter and picked up the next one.

'Harry was like a father to you, wasn't he?'

'Yep,' said Luke, snipping away at the hoof.

'Where's your real dad?'

Luke kept snipping for a while before he answered. 'Harry was my real dad.'

'I mean your biological dad.'

'Don't know, don't care,' Luke said in a neutral sort of voice.

He didn't offer anything more, and Jess wasn't sure whether to push it, because she couldn't see his face. She had never heard anything about Luke's real family, which was unusual in Coachwood Crossing. Everyone knew everything about everyone else in this town.

Luke silently cleaned, trimmed and filed the third hoof, and the fourth. When it was done, he dropped it and turned to face her, wiping the sweat off his forehead with his sleeve. 'How come you asked me that, about my real father?'

Jess shrugged and twiddled Dodger's forelock. 'I don't know.'

'My mum died when I was little and then my father adopted me out when I was four. When that didn't work out, I went into the foster system.'

61

Jess was stunned. 'Four? As in four years old?' She imagined Luke as a freckled four-year-old, with little four-year-old boots and four-year-old Wrangler jeans. He would have been so cute. 'Why?'

'I don't know. Because he's a loser.'

'So what happened to the people that fostered you?'

'Which ones?'

'How many *were* there?'

Luke didn't reply.

'You poor thing!' said Jess quietly.

'I can look after myself,' said Luke, sounding slightly defensive. 'Just because my old man's a dud, it doesn't mean I have to be. I've got a good job and I'll be able to buy a ute soon.' His voice lightened. 'An HQ. Then when Legsy and me win some big drafts, I'm gonna buy a property out west and run cattle.'

'How is Legs going?' she asked, letting the topic of Luke's father fall away.

'Good,' nodded Luke. He was being modest. Luke won everything on Legsy, and the colt was only a five-year-old.

'You ever gonna cut him?' asked Jess, pulling a carrot out of her pocket and taking a bite of it before giving the rest to Dodger.

'Not sure yet. Don't want to.' He winced in a way that made Jess laugh and reached out to pat Filth, who was trembling at his feet. The big dog jumped up and put his paws on Luke's shoulders, his tail waving clumsily back and forth.

'Taking Legsy droving?'

'Yep! One week to go!' He took Filth by the paws and started dancing with him, making Jess laugh again.

'Taking the dogs?'

'Nah, Lawson won't let them come. They're not cattle dogs, they'll just cause trouble.' He dropped Filth's paws and gave him a rub behind the ears.

'What about Tom?'

'He's hoping to come out for a few days later on. He's got a lot of study now he's at boarding school. Don't wanna get in the way of that. Lawson said he could ride Chocky, you know, the brumby I gave him? He's green broke now.'

Jess nodded. 'I saw Lawson riding Chocky the other day.'

'Wal's going too.'

'Wally?' Jess felt her hackles rise. 'Lawson better not break her in while he's got her out there. He promised me I could do that.'

'She's old enough to start, isn't she?'

'I already have, a bit.' Jess had been desensitising the filly to ropes for weeks. 'But don't tell Lawson that – he'll want to do it his way.'

'She's just going for the ride, I think,' said Luke. 'Why don't you come too?'

'I already asked. Dad freaked.'

'Couldn't talk him round, huh?'

'He reckons there are too many blokes going,' said Jess. 'It's no place for a *girl*.'

'He's probably right,' Luke said, giving her a cheeky smile. 'It's no place for a glam like you, Jessica Fairley.'

'What do you mean?' she asked, indignant.

'Nice shirt,' he commented.

Jess looked down at her scruffy red flannie, one of several she had pilfered from her father's wardrobe. They were comfy and warm and she didn't particularly care what they looked like. 'From the Craig Fairley collection,' she smiled, grabbing the shirt tails and curtseying.

'Guess it's the closest thing to a dress he'll ever see you in.'

'Yep,' said Jess, unapologetically. She looked him over. 'You can talk, Luke Matheson. You badly need a haircut.'

'There's some horse clippers in the tackroom.'

'Want me to do it now?'

'No.' Luke took a step back and placed his hat firmly on his head.

'I'm very neat,' Jess insisted. 'Just look at Dodger.'

Luke looked at Dodger's closely shaved mane and grimaced.

Lawson clomped down the path from Annie's house with some books tucked under his arm. 'Need a lift home, Jess? I'm going to see your dad.' He waved the books at her. 'Tax time!'

'Nah, I've got transport,' she answered, pointing to Dodger.

'You coming, Luke?'

'I'll ride over with Jess.'

Lawson smirked and got into his ute.

Jess ran after him. She pulled a bundle of notes out of her jeans pocket and dropped them into his lap. 'It's for Opal.'

He picked them up and handed them back to her. 'Not yet.'

'But I want to pay for her.'

Lawson pushed the money back at her and shook his head. 'See how she goes out on the station first.'

'I don't want to send her out there, she's not well enough,' said Jess.

'It'd be the best thing for her,' said Lawson. 'She needs to be with a mob of horses. If you try handling her while she's got an attitude like that, you'll end up with one dangerous horse. She'll turn out just like that crazy white thing.'

Jess shook her head. She had made her decision. 'She's not going without me.'

Lawson wrapped two large hands around hers, enclosing the money firmly inside. 'Yes, she is — because I still own her.'

Jess stared at him, her mouth agape. His face was closed and hard. She had seen that impenetrable will on his face before. When she could finally speak, she said, 'You . . . absolute . . . *pig!*'

7

JESS LAY AWAKE in bed, furiously grinding her jaw back and forth. She'd spent all week trying to convince her parents to intervene, to demand Lawson hand over her filly, but they refused. He owned Opal and there was nothing they could or would do to change that.

But there was just no way she was letting Lawson take Opal out west without her. Opal was weaned, and that meant she was *her* filly, money or no money.

Jess lay restlessly for what seemed an eternity, listening to her parents' banter in the kitchen and the babble of the television behind their words. Finally, she heard intermittent snaps around the house as the lights were turned out and the TV was silenced for the night.

Beneath her bed was a fat backpack containing a change of clothes, a jacket, a torch, a pair of pliers, a drink bottle and a riding helmet, plus her entire savings – including the money for Opal. A handwritten note for her parents was in the side pocket.

A thread of guilt wove through Jess's anger. She couldn't believe she was about to do this to her parents. But when the house fell completely still and she could hear the steady whistle of her father's snoring, she reached below her bed and pulled out a pair of jeans and a jumper. She wriggled into them under her quilt, so as not to make any creaking sounds on the timber floorboards, then lay still again. When all remained quiet, she rose, grabbed her backpack and tiptoed to the toilet.

She stood staring at the four walls for the appropriate length of time, tore some paper off the roll and flushed it down the loo. Then she tiptoed back along the hallway, placing her note on the hat rack on the way.

Dear Mum and Dad,

If I let her go with Lawson, I'll never see her again. Please don't be mad at me.

Love, Jess.

Instead of turning into her room, Jess continued five more steps to the back door, stooped to pick up her boots and ever so slowly turned the knob. She sneaked across the garden in her socks. It was a clear night and the half-moon cast an eerie glow over the yards. The night air was soft and moist. Guilty as she felt, she did love a night ride.

'Good boy, Dodger,' she whispered as she neared the yard. She fetched her saddle, slung it over his back and tied her swag behind. Then she slipped on his bridle and led him out into the grazing paddock. If she rode him along the road her parents might hear the hoofbeats. She would cut through the paddock, along the river flats towards town and then up the road to Harry's place. Luckily, Dodger was unshod and his footsteps wouldn't clang too much.

A cool breeze tickled the back of her neck, bringing smells of freshly slashed grass with it. She drew alongside the Broadhead property, which was mostly bushland and tall forest. It had trails going through to the main road, but she didn't know them well enough to avoid the house. And the Broadhead family had yappy little terriers that would certainly let the whole town know if someone was snooping around. Tegan Broadhead was Katrina's best friend, and would jump at the chance to dob Jess in.

She rode until she came to the bridge that led into town. There was an old drover's gate from years ago that Lawson had told her about, hidden somewhere in the trees, which would help her bypass town. She found it without too much fuss, aided by her torch. Beyond it was the road that led to Annie and Harry's place.

Before she got to the front gate, she slipped off Dodger and quietly called up the dogs. Filth and Fang would go off their heads if they heard a stranger at the gate. Filth instantly recognised her voice and bounded towards her, almost bowling her over. Fang growled a low growl, unsure of the midnight visitor.

'Fang,' she whispered, holding out a hand. 'It's just me.'

He sniffed her hand and then pushed his ears into her hand for a scratch.

On the side of the road, on a grassy strip, a ute was loaded with hay, saddles and droving gear. She knew Luke planned to leave before sunrise and catch up with Lawson, who had left the previous evening. Luke would be waking within hours, loading Legsy onto the float and heading for mulga country.

Jess looked to the round yard where Opal and the brumbies had been. It was empty. Lawson must have taken Opal. She was on her way to Blakely Downs. Jess tethered Dodger to the side of the truck and rolled out her swag, then nestled down with the dogs curled up next to her.

Sleep didn't come to her as easily as she imagined it would, and she lay there restlessly, listening to the cars driving down that road in the wee hours and wondering where they were going or coming from. Each time one passed she curled up smaller in her swag and hoped no one would think it odd or suspicious that Dodger was tied to the front fence in the middle of the night.

In between cars, the noises at Harry's were much like the night noises at home: bats screeching and hovering in the sky like big black birds, crickets chirruping and wind rustling at the trees.

Jess tried to imagine what Luke's reaction would be when he found her. He'd get a surprise, all right.

Dodger's nickering made her sit up. Footsteps crunched through the dark, along the gravel driveway and through the front gate. The dogs leapt from Jess's side and cool air replaced their patches of cosy warmth. Metal jingled as the gate latch was removed and replaced.

'Who's there?' Luke asked in a cautious tone, pushing away the dogs as they danced excitedly around his feet.

'It's only me,' Jess whispered back as she unzipped her swag.

'Hello, only me,' he said, sounding curious but wary.

'It's *me*, Jess.'

'Yeah, I know.' Luke still sounded puzzled. ''What are you doing in there?'

'I'm coming to Longwood. Can you fit Dodger on the float?' Jess let herself off the back of the ute.

'Why didn't you just come up to the flat?'

'I didn't want Annie to hear me.'

'Why not?'

'Umm, I haven't told anyone that I'm going.'

'Why not?'

'Because they won't let me go,' she whispered.

'Jess . . .'

'There's no *way* I'm letting Lawson throw Opal onto a station to just live or die,' she hissed. 'She's *my* filly, not his, and he's got no right to take her!'

'He still owns her, doesn't—'

'He does *not* still own her!' Jess squeaked. 'We had an agreement! As soon as Opal was weaned, she was *mine*. If he won't take the money for her, then that's his own stupid fault. He's taken *my* filly!'

'He just doesn't want to sell you a dud horse, Jessy—'

'*A dud horse?*' Jess wanted to punch something.

Fang rushed suddenly to Luke's side. He sank to his haunches and let out a low menacing snarl.

The sound shocked her and she took a step back.

'It's okay, boy,' said Luke, putting a hand on the dog's head. 'He doesn't like it when people get aggro with me . . . especially with no good reason.'

Jess took a deep breath and willed herself to calm down. 'I'm not angry with *you*,' she said, her voice beginning to quaver. Then she said through her teeth,

'I'm angry at *Lawson*.' She could barely say his name.

There was an awkward silence, which was soon broken by a confused whimper from Filth. He sidled up to Jess and shoved at her hand with his wet nose. She dropped to one knee and buried her face in his woolly coat, and he wiggled appreciatively.

'I think Lawson also might be worried about the reputation of his mare,' said Luke. 'He should be able to get a lot of money for her foals down the track.'

'So he's worried that Opal might be bad advertising,' said Jess bitterly.

Luke shrugged.

Jess shook her head.

'He's trying to do the right thing by you, too.'

'*What?*' said Jess with disbelief. 'He's taken my filly – which I've waited more than eighteen months for – and you think he's trying to do the right thing by me?' She threw her hands in the air. 'Why does everyone always stick up for him? Grace is right: the men in your family *are* chauvinists!'

Luke folded his arms across his chest and said nothing.

Tears of frustration rolled down Jess's cheeks. 'Are you going to let me come droving or not?'

'I can't.'

'No, of course not,' said Jess, icily.

'I think you'd be crazy to run away from your parents.

73

And I don't want you to use me to do it. I could lose my job.'

'I thought you wanted me to come.'

'Not like this.'

'*You* did it. You ran away.'

'It wasn't the same.'

Jess was silent. She was too teary and choked up to speak anymore.

'I'm gonna go and grab Legsy from the stable.' Luke's feet crunched away over the gravel and his form was swallowed up by the night.

8

JESS RODE BACK UP her own driveway just as the sun was rising. Ripping the saddle from Dodger's back, she threw it on the ground. She opened the gate into the paddock for him, then hurled her bridle at the saddle as she walked towards the house.

Caroline came running down the steps with the phone in one hand and a crumpled piece of paper in the other. 'Yes, Annie, it's her. She's home. Thank God for that . . . Yes . . . Yep . . . Bye, Annie, thanks. And sorry to have bothered you so early in the morning.'

She turned to Jess. 'Jessica, what the hell are you playing at? I've rung half the town trying to find you. We've been worried sick.' She stopped and looked at her daughter. 'What happened? Are you okay?'

Jess didn't look up from the ground in front of her.

'Don't ever, *ever* do that to me again, do you hear me?' Caroline put her arms around Jess's heaving shoulders, and swore as she rubbed her back. Craig came marching across the front garden but his wife held up a hand. He surveyed the situation, did an about-turn and went back up the steps.

'Everyone's sticking up for Lawson,' Jess cried, wiping her nose on Caroline's dressing-gown sleeve. 'They think Opal's a dud horse. They're just going to let her go out onto a station and die.'

'Crikey, Jess,' said her mother. 'It's one thing for a foal to die, but it's entirely another for you to. Anything could have happened to you. How the hell did you intend to get to Blakely Downs on your own?'

'I was going to go with Luke.' Jess started sobbing. 'But he wouldn't take me. He's mad at me.'

'You can't drag other people into your troubles,' said Caroline. 'He was right to send you back home.'

'But *he* did it. *He* ran away,' sobbed Jess. 'I thought he would understand.'

'Luke was a troubled kid, Jess. You can't begin to compare his life with yours.'

'No, because he's a boy and I'm a girl!' said Jess angrily. 'He comes home a hero and gets given an expensive colt, and I get my filly taken off me!'

'He's also two years older than you, Jess.'

'No, he's not. I'm nearly sixteen.'

'You're not sixteen yet, Miss Fairley, and you're most certainly too young to be driving off around the outback with an older boy. Especially one with a past like Luke's.'

'What do you mean by *that*?'

'He's a wild boy with a wild past,' said Caroline. 'I'm worried about this friendship you have with him, Jess. I don't like it.'

'Why?' demanded Jess. 'Just because he has no parents? You pretend to be all open-minded and peace, love and lentils, but you're not. You're as judgemental as anyone else. You're such a hypocrite!'

'He's violent, Jess.'

'He is *not*,' said Jess, raising her voice. 'He's the most *un*violent person I know!

'I just want you to be careful,' said Caroline.

'Well, you don't have to worry about him anymore because he *hates my guts*,' Jess screamed as loudly as she could. She stormed past her mother, flew up the stairs of the house and slammed herself inside her room with a thunderous crash of her door.

As she threw herself onto the bed she ripped her phone from her pocket and began thumbing a text message to Shara, Grace and Rosie.

I hate all men!!!!!

Within minutes, it buzzed back at her.

Grace: join the club.

Shara: omg, Ws^?

Rosie: Huh?

Lawsons taken opal, he wont sell her 2 me,
luke stuck ^ 4 him, we had a fight.

Buzz, buzz, buzz, rumble.

Grace: yep, the boys always stick together,
told you!!!

Shara: omg, why? when? what did luke say?

Rosie: What time is it???

Luke wouldnt take me droving, said opals a dud,
bad advertising for marnie, theyr all misogynists,
if opal was a colt theyd save her!

Jess's phone began having epileptic fits in her hand.

Grace: told u they r all pigs!

Shara: omg! I can't believe he said that!
Rosie: wotz a misogynist? too early, head hurts,
groan.

Buzz, buzz, rumble.

Grace: they r all girl haters – derrr rosie!

Rosie: shut up dog breath.

I'm never gona c opal again ☹ ☹ ☹

That afternoon, Jess lay on her bed listening to the
angriest music she could find on her iPod and thinking
about Luke out droving, male, as free as a bird, and with
no parents to tell him what he could and couldn't do.

Over pauses in the music, she heard the persistent ring
of the phone and a muffled conversation. Seconds later,
her door opened and her mother stood there mouthing
something.

'What?'

Caroline leaned over the bed and plucked out Jess's earplugs. 'Come to the kitchen and have a talk with us for a minute.'

In the kitchen, her parents sat at the table looking grave. 'Come and sit down, honey,' said Caroline. 'Judy Arnold just rang.'

Jess felt her breathing slow. 'What for?' Grace and Rosie's crazy mum never rang this house. 'What's wrong?'

Craig exhaled thoughtfully and looked at his wife, as if to clarify that they were in consensus.

'What?' Jess became increasingly worried. 'Is it Rosie or Grace? What? What's happened?'

'She's going out to Blakely Downs with the girls to join Lawson and Ryan,' said Craig.

Jess's jaw dropped. 'Grace and Rosie too? You're kidding me!' She groaned, then quickly geared up for a rant. '*Everyone gets to go but me!* My filly is thrown out in the middle of nowhere with no one to look after her, and everyone is just going off chasing cows!'

'Well, they've invited you to go too,' said Caroline.

Jess swallowed her rant, unsure if she'd heard right.

Her mother nodded.

Jess folded her arms. 'And let me guess – I'm not allowed to go. I have to go and do karmic yoga sessions under the full moon for six months until I can *nurture my anger with love!*'

'It's only for ten days over the holidays. I'm sure we can postpone the yoga until you get back,' Caroline said dryly.

'You're letting me go?'

'Well, as we said earlier,' said Craig, 'if there wasn't just a bunch of men out there, we'd be more likely to consider it. With a responsible woman to chaperone you, then maybe . . .'

'You'll be away for your birthday,' said Caroline.

'I'm *going*?'

Caroline smiled and nodded.

Jess screamed and threw her arms around her mother. Then she leapt from the chair and did a dance around the kitchen. 'I'm going to Blakely Downs! I can find Opal and bring her back.' She paused and looked at her mum. 'How will I get Dodger out there?'

'He's not going.'

'Why not? Who will I ride?'

'You're not riding.'

'Not riding?'

'You'll be cooking and helping Mrs Arnold to pack up and move camp,' said Craig.

Jess gave a sardonic laugh. 'Of course.'

'That is the only way we'll allow you to go, Jessica,' said her father. 'You will be under her strict supervision.'

'This trip is not about Opal,' said Caroline. 'You'll be

on the road with the cattle. She'll be turned out on the station somewhere. I doubt you'll even see her.'

Jess let her mother's words float in one ear, waft around and then sail out the other. She would find a way to bring Opal home. 'Grace was so right,' she said, changing the subject. 'Boys get to do all the fun stuff.'

'You're not going out there for a holiday, Jess. Droving is hard work and long hours. Lawson is expecting you to work. His horses will be working hard too, moving cattle all day, so I doubt you'll be riding much,' her father repeated. 'Even if you stay in one spot for a few days, there'll still be meals to cook and jobs to do.'

'I know, I know, I'll work really hard,' said Jess, her mind already plotting.

'Oh, and there's one more thing,' said Caroline.

'What?' Jess broke from her scheming. 'Is there a catch?'

'Shara is going too.'

'*Yesss!*' Jess couldn't believe her luck. 'Are Shara and Rosie and Grace taking their horses?'

'Nope, you're all going in the car with Mrs Arnold.'

Jess slumped. 'Well, that'll make it difficult.' How would she ride back to the station to find Opal?

'I don't see why,' said Caroline. 'You won't need a horse to pack camp and cook.'

'Oh yeah,' smiled Jess, brushing it off. 'Course not!'

'And don't you even think of sneaking off with Luke, young lady.'

'I wouldn't!' said Jess, incensed.

But with Opal I might . . .

Caroline scoffed. 'You just did, Jessica. You scared the life out of me. If you *dare* do that to Mrs Arnold, I've told her she is to send you straight home.'

'I promise I won't, Mum.'

'You'd better not,' Caroline reiterated. 'I'm serious, Jess. If you don't do exactly what Mrs Arnold says, you'll be on the first train home.'

'I *will*, I *won't*,' groaned Jess. Then *she* was suddenly serious. She looked at her dad. 'Will you take care of Dodger for me while I'm gone?'

'Sure,' he nodded. 'Come on, we'll go down to the shed and you can show me everything I need to do.' Jess could tell he was fighting the urge to look happy for her. She didn't mind, though; she knew looking grave and apprehensive about your daughter's crazy plans was considered the proper parental thing to do.

9

JUDY ARNOLD DIDN'T BOTHER to slow down for the potholes in the driveway. The headlights threw wild streaks of light around the front yard as she barrelled the chunky LandCruiser along at full speed, jamming on the brakes just as Jess thought it would career straight through the house. With the engine still running, she swung out of the driver's side door, wearing thongs, jeans and an oilskin jacket.

Jess jumped off her packed duffle bag and hauled it down the front steps. 'Just wait, Mrs Arnold,' she called as she ran to the packing shed. 'Mum donated some veggies.' She grabbed the cardboard box by the doorway and carried it back to the four-wheel drive. 'Reckon it'll fit?'

Mrs Arnold looked at the box suspiciously. 'We usually dehydrate stuff like that,' she said. 'It'll go off pretty quick.'

'It's just a couple of days' worth. Mum's worried I'll get scurvy.' Although Jess knew it to be a ploy by mothers everywhere, Caroline had done a particularly good job instilling in her a fear of spongy gums and bleeding lips.

'Shove it in somewhere and let's get going,' said Mrs Arnold.

Jess wrestled the box in with the luggage and slammed the door. She dived into the back and threw her arms around Shara's neck. 'I'm so stoked you could come!'

'Wouldn't miss it.' Shara gave her a squeeze, then whispered, 'Let's find Opal!'

The vehicle took off up the driveway.

'Seatbelts!' roared Mrs Arnold above the noise of the engine.

Jess hung her head out the window and waved to Caroline and Craig, who stood in their robes on the front verandah, looking bleary-eyed in the gentle rising of the day.

Grace leaned over and turned up the music. 'Woohoo! Let's get some road behind us!'

They reached Blakely Downs late in the afternoon. The station seemed little more than a set of yards built from metal poles, with a jumble of covered shelters behind them. There were long, shallow water troughs, cattle ramps and big metal hay feeders. A shed large enough to house an aeroplane sat beyond the yards, with old drums, spare tyres and assorted hoses and farm equipment scattered about. Timber pallets were loaded with sacks of fertiliser and other miscellaneous farm supplies. Several cattle crates were parked alongside the shed and the nose of a large bulldozer poked out from a wide doorway. In a distant yard, a few small, scruffy horses took shelter from the blistering sun under a stringy sapling.

'Hey, that's Rusty,' said Jess, leaning over Shara to get a look out the opposite window. The little red brumby with his thick shaggy tail was unmistakeable. 'Oh my God, look! There's Tinks! They haven't turned them out yet!' Jess opened the door. 'Opal must be here too!'

'At least let me stop before you get out,' said Mrs Arnold, as Jess suspended one leg out of the vehicle. 'If you'll just hang on, I'll drive over there.'

Jess held the door ajar as they rumbled over the lumpy ground to the small yard. She strained to see into the yards, and was out and running before Mrs Arnold had the handbrake on.

'Opal,' she called, as she took hold of the top rail and peered under it. 'Where are you, girl?' Tinks and Rusty swished their tails and flicked an ear in her direction. 'I can't see her. Where is she? *Opal!*'

A man in jeans and a big hat walked out of the huge shed and strode towards her with a piece of greasy machinery and an old rag in his hands. Jess recognised his dark, familiar face with its neatly trimmed beard – it was the stockman who'd offered to buy Dodger at the Longwood campdraft.

'Bob, where's the foal?' Mrs Arnold demanded, her thongs slapping as she walked to the yards.

The stockman pointed to the other end of the yard, where a small brown lump lay lifelessly in the sun, camouflaged by a coating of dust. 'Sleeping.'

'Grace reckons it's got a spastic head. Is that right?' Mrs Arnold folded her body over and let herself through the fence.

Jess glared at Grace, who held up her hands in innocence.

Bob nodded gravely, as he rubbed at the thing in his hands.

'Be careful, she attacks people,' warned Jess, climbing up onto the fence.

'So does Mum,' Grace sniggered.

Mrs Arnold gave her daughter a look of thunder, then turned to Jess. 'Want me to look at the horse or not?'

Jess looked to Rosie.

'It's okay, she knows what she's doing,' her friend reassured her. 'Come and sit on the fence and watch.'

Judy Arnold marched over to where Opal lay, then continued walking straight past her.

The filly startled and scrambled to her feet. She whinnied as she galloped to the other horses, who whinnied back and trotted to meet her.

'They're looking after her,' said Jess. It was a touching sight. Opal nuzzled into Rusty's side and Tinks came around from behind, circling her.

Mrs Arnold turned and walked past Opal again. As she did, Opal flattened her ears and broke from the mob, rushing at her.

The woman spun to face her, looked directly into her eyes and yelled '*BAAAH!*' so loudly that Jess nearly fell off the fence. Opal stopped in her tracks and stared like a startled possum.

For a brief moment, the woman and the scrawny foal locked eyes, until Mrs Arnold waved her arms and yelled, 'Gwahn! Get!' Opal scuttled off to the other horses and Mrs Arnold turned her back and walked off. Opal trotted out and lunged at the intruder again, but Mrs Arnold spun around, and drove her away once more.

'It's got *debil debil* in its head, that one,' said Bob.

Jess spun and glared at him.

He nodded at her. 'How's Dodger? You wanna sell that old fulla yet?'

Jess shook her head. 'Sorry.'

Bob gestured at Opal in the camp. 'That horse is from the min mins. She got *debil debil* in her head. I told Lawson.'

'She's not Lawson's horse, she's mine,' Jess corrected him. 'And she's not a dud, if that's what you're trying to say.'

In the yards, Mrs Arnold kept pushing Opal away, and the more she did so, the more Opal came at her – or *to* her, Jess realised. It was hard to tell when the turnaround happened. After several more clashes, Mrs Arnold allowed Opal to follow for a few paces. Then she bent and lowered herself to the ground, sitting on one heel, with her hands crossed easily over her knee.

Opal dropped her crooked head and sniffed the back of her neck, and, without looking at her, Mrs Arnold reached back to give her a gentle rub. As though in a trance, Opal closed her eyes and rested her muzzle on the woman's shoulder.

'You do need some help, don't you, little one,' Mrs Arnold murmured as she stroked the bony forehead.

'Pretty cool, huh?' Rosie whispered to Jess.

'That is amazing,' whispered Jess in awe. 'No one has ever been able to get near her without tranquillising her first.'

Shara gave Jess an excited squeeze. 'Maybe her head's getting better!'

Jess turned to Bob. 'See? No *debil debil*!'

Bob continued polishing the thing in his hand. His expression didn't change.

Mrs Arnold let the foal be and walked back towards the LandCruiser. Jess ran after her. 'How did you do that, Mrs Arnold? No one has ever been able to get near her before.'

'I just talked to her on her own terms,' said Mrs Arnold. 'Not that she had anything nice to say. Come on, we have to get going. Jump in.'

Jess turned to Bob. 'Who's looking after the horses back here?'

'Oh, plenty of fullas to look after them, lots of staff. The *debil* horse stays at the homestead till Lawson gets back and makes sure she's okay before he lets her out onto the station.' He stared knowingly at Jess. 'Said life wouldn't be worth living if anything happened to her.'

'He got that bit right,' said Jess. 'So what if anything happens when we're out droving?'

'They got Lawson's number. They'll call if she goes downhill.'

Jess ran to the four-wheel drive, scrawled her mobile number on the back of a scrap of paper and dashed back to Bob. 'Can you tell them that this is the number to ring if anything happens to that filly? They're to ring me, not Lawson.'

Bob gave her an uneasy look.

'*I'm* the owner. They need to ring *me*,' Jess repeated, shoving the piece of paper at him.

Bob looked at Mrs Arnold. 'Who owns the horse?'

Mrs Arnold shrugged. 'Lawson did promise it to her.'

Bob hesitantly took the number and walked back to the shed with it.

Jess squeezed into the LandCruiser with the other girls, her neck craned back to the yards. She felt a lifting of the heaviness she had been carrying, a sudden sense of hope. Mrs Arnold's link-up with Opal was only a small step, but it was a forward one.

'Hopping on, Bob?' yelled Mrs Arnold, as she started the engine.

Bob emerged from the shed, slinging a small pack over his shoulder, and jumped onto the running board that ran along the side of the four-wheel drive. He banged twice on the roof and Mrs Arnold shoved the vehicle into first and took off.

Jess stuck her head out the window. 'Are you coming droving too?'

Bob nodded. 'Horse tailer – my favourite job!'

10

THEY REACHED THE CAMP just as the sun was setting. Jess was relieved. If she had to listen to her friends sing the Kasey Chambers pony song one more time, she was going to have an aneurism.

The country was dotted with mulga trees and tufts of Mitchell grass, which Jess knew were filled with nutritional goodness despite a wiry, outwardly parched appearance. A gooseneck trailer towed by Lawson's ute was parked by the side of a dirt track; a chunky stockman in black jeans tended the fire; tethered horses swished their tails, and motorbikes, scattered saddles and cooking equipment were strewn about. Another ute, old and yellow and missing the driver's door, was parked nearby with a motorbike in the back.

Between the camp and the burning sunset, a large mob of cows were boxed inside a break that was fenced off with two strands of electric tape. Stretching away in the other direction, a separate ring of electric wires enclosed twenty or so horses as they chewed on the day's grain rations. There were dogs everywhere: mostly big kelpies, plus a couple of heavy-jawed Smithfield cattle dogs chained to trees, panting.

'Hey Jess, there's Walkabout,' said Grace.

Jess beamed. 'Wally!' Amid the horses, she could make out Walkabout's spotted white rump. She ran her eyes over the filly, checking for saddle marks, and was relieved to find none.

Lawson stepped out of a side door in the trailer and walked out to meet them. Jess set her jaw hard and stared fiercely at him.

'My dear Aunty Jude,' he said, ignoring Jess.

'Don't give me that Dear Aunty routine,' Mrs Arnold said dryly, but with the faintest hint of a smile.

Lawson peered into the back of the LandCruiser, where the girls were unclipping seatbelts and crawling over each other. 'I see you brought the hired help along,' he said.

'You didn't think you could ditch this lot that easily, did you?'

'Thought it was worth a try.' Lawson pulled a face at Grace, who stuck a finger up at him.

'The girls stay in the trailer with me, and if one of them grubby ringers so much as looks at 'em, I'll knock his block off.' Mrs Arnold turned around to the girls and snapped, 'And I'll do the same to you lot, you hear?'

The girls all straightened and nodded attentively. All, that is, except Grace, who made a half-hearted attempt to stifle a giggle.

'Do you hear me, Grace Arnold?' her mother shouted so loudly that Jess winced and the black-jeaned man looked over at the commotion.

'Yes, Mum.'

Lawson roared with laughter. 'It'd be a brave man who'd mess with your daughters, Jude.'

'Where's Lindy?' asked Mrs Arnold.

'Gone into town to organise permits and get some supplies. She'll be back later tonight,' said Lawson. 'Come on over.'

'What about me husband?'

'Stanley's hiding back at the river. Made some excuse about checking for dingos.'

'Hmph,' said Mrs Arnold, and planted her foot on the accelerator. Lawson stepped hastily out of the way.

Before the girls had a chance to stretch their legs from the long drive, Lawson set about giving orders. 'Jess, there are two horses tied up that need unsaddling and a rub-down. Make sure you do a good job; they've had more than six hours under a saddle today. Put 'em in the break with the others when you're done.' He issued further instructions as he walked. 'Then you can feed the dogs. There's a bag of dry food under the trailer.'

Jess set to work without speaking to him.

By late in the evening, the workers had all had a sustaining meal and the girls had washed dishes, kneaded dough for the next day's bread, collected firewood, lugged water, made billy tea and semi-prepared the next morning's breakfast.

Jess stood next to Shara by an open fire, a large helping of potatoes and meat sitting in her stomach. The fire was blistering hot on her face and arms while the descending night wrapped a blanket of icy cold around her back and shoulders. She turned herself slowly like a rotisserie, trying to even out the warmth.

'Did Luke say hello to you?' asked Shara. She scooped a hunk of potato into her mouth.

Jess rubbed her hands together over the flames. 'Nope.'

'He probably just hasn't had a chance yet. He looked pretty busy.'

'Yeah, whatever,' said Jess. 'I didn't come out here to see him.'

'He's over there by the goosey,' said Shara, nodding towards the trailer.

'Yes. I know,' said Jess curtly. She was painfully aware of Luke's whereabouts, after deliberately avoiding him all evening. She changed the subject. 'Did you meet the ringers?'

'Yeah,' said Shara.

Rosie appeared from the shadows and sat on a log with a plate of steaming food. 'Are they hot?' she whispered.

Shara made a face as if she had just choked on her own vomit. 'They're really old, probably in their thirties or something. The stumpy one's called Dave and the scrawny one's called Clarkey.'

Grace joined them with a cup of hot Milo. 'They're Ryan's loser mates. Mum reckons Lindy's not very happy about them coming.'

Rosie sighed and arranged her potatoes in a row on her plate. 'Bummer,' she said, poking her fork into one, inspecting it and then placing it neatly into her mouth. 'You'll have to share Luke with us, Jessy,' she giggled.

'He's not mine to share.'

'Are you kidding me? He's totally in love with you!' said Rosie.

'We're just friends.'

'So if he went off with Katrina Pettilow, you wouldn't care?'

'I wouldn't like it if *any*one went off with Katrina,' snapped Jess.

Rosie raised her eyebrows. 'Touchy.'

Jess walked over to a log and plonked herself down without answering.

Shara sat next to her and gave her a friendly nudge. 'Come on, Jessy,' she said quietly. 'Look where we are! Opal's going to be fine. They've got your number, so you'll soon get a message if she's not. Let's enjoy ourselves.'

Jess thawed a little and nudged her back. 'I'm sorry,' she said. 'I just can't stop thinking about her. I hate not having control of her. I feel as if Lawson's going to take her from me, just like he did with Wally.'

'You'll feel better once you get some sleep. It probably won't be so busy tomorrow,' said Shara. 'We'll just sit on the horses and watch the cattle graze.'

'Hope we can sleep in a bit,' said Jess.

That fantasy was quickly shattered. 'You girls had better hit the sack. We'll be up at four.' Mrs Arnold bent down and picked up their plates and cups. 'Roll out your swags in the trailer.'

'Four?' Jess and Shara stared at each other in horror. *'In the morning?'*

'I'll die,' said Rosie from the other side of the fire.

Jess got up and followed Mrs Arnold back into the trailer. 'Can we sleep outside under the stars, Mrs Arnold?'

'No,' was the short reply. Mrs Arnold dropped a stack of dirty tin cups and cutlery into a large plastic bowl.

A small battery-powered lamp hung from the ceiling, casting feeble shadows around the inside of the trailer. In the neck, beyond all the bags of food, tangles of leather and miscellaneous kitchen items, was a large shelf, broad enough for three to lie comfortably across. Four would be a squeeze but Jess was too tired to care.

'All of us have to sleep up here,' said Grace, scrambling into the peak and poking her head over the edge.

'I'm not sleeping next to you in those filthy clothes,' Rosie whined. 'Mum, make Grace get changed. She stinks.'

'At least take your jeans off, Grace,' said Mrs Arnold in a disinterested tone. 'They're covered in cow dung.'

'Fine,' said Grace, ripping them off and throwing them at her sister's head. Rosie ducked and Jess copped a face full of rancid denim that smelled as though it hadn't left Grace's body for a week. To add insult to injury, the metal button clouted her in the eye.

'Crikey, Grace!' she grumbled as she clutched her face.

Grace winced. 'Sorry, Jess!'

'Oh, for Pete's sake!' yelled Mrs Arnold. 'Will you girls sort yourselves out and get to bed?'

The girls shut up and quickly set about their sleeping arrangements.

'She's caged us in for the night,' whispered Rosie as they wriggled into their bedding.

'Surprised she hasn't put bars over the windows,' Grace whispered back.

On the floor of the trailer, Mrs Arnold had unfolded a stretcher bed for herself midway between the door and the girls.

Jess snuggled into her sleeping bag and flipped open her phone, checking for messages from the station. She wouldn't be able to sleep unless she knew Opal was okay. There was one new message.

Luke: bout time you got out here!

Jess couldn't control the huge grin that spread over her face. At least Luke wasn't mad at her anymore. She flipped the phone shut and fell asleep holding it snug in her hand.

11

IT SEEMED HER HEAD had only just hit the pillow when Jess felt her toe being pulled. The timber floor clunked as Mrs Arnold moved about.

'Time to get up, girls. Gotta get everybody fed before sun-up,' she said.

Grace was already up and dressed in her noisome jeans, looking as though she'd never been to bed. 'Come on, Jess,' she said excitedly. 'If we get brekky done in time, we can help count out the cattle.' She opened the side door and stepped into the darkness. 'I'll stoke the fire,' she told her mother through the narrow doorway. 'Will we do the bread in the camp oven?'

Mrs Arnold's homemade bread was legendary. Grace had told Jess how she baked it in a huge cast-iron pot with a lid that she buried in the coals of the fire. It had to be done just right or the crust would burn. When it was done properly, Grace reckoned it was all anyone needed for breakfast, lunch and dinner. Nothing tasted better. Jess had helped make the dough the night before, kneading until her arms nearly fell off. They'd left the silky smooth warm bundles under tea towels for the morning and now she was looking forward to tasting the finished product.

'I'll be out in a minute, Grace,' said Mrs Arnold. She turned to the others, who were still trying to come to terms with the day. 'Get dressed and roll up those sleeping bags.' Then she squeezed out the door after her daughter. 'Where's your father?'

There was a tapping sound on the small curved window of the gooseneck and Rosie rolled over and lifted the curtain. Outside, Stanley Arnold gave a cheeky wave and held his finger to his lips. Rosie giggled. Her dad had been AWOL since they arrived.

As Stanley waved and pulled faces, two hands came from nowhere and wrapped around his throat. His expression quickly changed as Mrs Arnold dragged him away by the neck. 'Where did you get to last night?' they heard her say.

'Poor Dad,' said Rosie, giggling. 'Mum's really going to give it to him.' She fought her way out of the confusion of blankets, pillows and sleeping bags and leapt to the floor. Jess and Shara followed, bumping into each other as they rummaged through their bags in the half-light to find their clothes.

Outside, the camp was still and the air was crisp and cold. Not far away, the cows lay under the small mulga trees inside the break, peacefully chewing their cud. The embers of the previous night's fire glowed softly and a discarded chair lay on its back.

A camping table had been set up just outside the trailer door and under Mrs Arnold's command, Jess set about helping with the bread, stirring the coals into life, mixing milk powder, making tea, and frying eggs and bacon in a cast-iron pan the size of a car tyre. She added some of her mother's mushrooms and cherry tomatoes to the pan. With her hands wrapped in a towel, she took it off the heat and placed it, still sizzling, onto a breadboard on the camping table. She laid some fresh asparagus on top to warm through.

The sleepy orange light of early morning grew stronger and hotter as the camp came to life. Car doors slammed and horses whinnied for their feed. The cattle began to bellow and a thousand birds welcomed the day with their song. The men swung saddles over their mounts and the cattle milled around the end of the break, eager to get out and feed. They'd been on the road for more than a week and knew the routine well. They would feed and graze along the stock route, and water at the designated water point around lunchtime.

One by one, the men gathered hungrily around the table and began helping themselves to breakfast. A small woman in dusty moleskins came over, leading a sooty dun horse. She looked neat and organised, with her dark hair pulled back into a ponytail beneath a cap and her shirt tucked in. Her face was deeply tanned and her eyes were liquid black. Two blue Smithfields panted at her heels.

'Morning. I'm Lindy Wright,' she said, holding out a hand to Jess. 'Harry and my dad were business partners. They owned Blakely Downs together.'

'Hi, I'm Jess.' Jess shook the woman's hand. 'Harry was a friend of mine.'

Lindy scooped an egg and some bacon and mushrooms onto a chunk of bread, avoiding the asparagus. 'I think I saw you at his funeral. You put the stockhorse tie on his casket, right?'

Jess suddenly recognised her. 'The black lacy—'

Lindy chuckled. 'That's one part of Harry's history that he never lived down.'

Jess looked at her questioningly.

'He did a striptease at a fundraiser for the local fire brigade.' Lindy rolled her eyes. 'Funniest day of my life. They auctioned the bra afterwards – cost me a week's wages.'

'He didn't . . .'

'Came dangerously close,' laughed Lindy. 'Wasn't pretty.'

Jess grimaced.

'Lindy!' Rosie squealed and jumped all over the woman like an excited puppy.

Lindy gave her a huge hug. 'Hi, Rosie!' she said cheerfully. 'How good is this? Better than sticking them on trucks, ay?'

'I reckon,' said Grace, muscling in for a hug.

'Watch my brekky,' Lindy laughed, holding her egg roll up in the air. Rosie and Grace backed off a little but kept chattering excitedly.

'Thanks for letting us come,' said Rosie.

Lindy smiled. 'Harry'd be stoked to know you all were out here with his cattle. He took me on this route every year when I was a kid. He was the only bloke in town who'd let a girl ride.'

'Shame his son's not like that,' Jess blurted without thinking.

'Hey?'

'Lawson doesn't let girls do anything.'

'Lawson does what I tell him to,' said Lindy matter-of-factly.

Rosie whispered in Jess's ear. 'Lindy's the boss drover. She's got Lawson . . .' She twirled an invisible piece of string around her finger.

Jess stared at the petite woman who reportedly had Lawson Blake wrapped around her little finger. She wondered if that could be true, and if so, *what her secret was*.

'Work hard, listen up and learn as much as you can,' said Lindy. 'If you do a good job and don't complain, Lawson'll give you all the respect you deserve; no more, no less.' She bit into her breakfast. 'So will I, for that matter.'

Jess listened as Lindy went over last-minute directions with Mrs Arnold, letting her know where the dinner camp would be. She had arranged to water the cattle at a private bore on one of the nearby stations, with easy road access. A little way beyond that was a good clear area with a few trees where the men and cattle could rest for a couple of hours.

'Hmm, good feed,' Lindy said, licking at her fingers. She nodded to Mrs Arnold. 'Thanks for coming out, Judy. We'll catch up tonight, ay?'

Judy Arnold smiled warmly. 'See you later on, love.' It was the first time Jess had seen a softer side of her; towards people, anyway.

Lindy turned and looked at one of the ringers who lurked nearby, his face obscured by his hat. 'Sun's up, Clarkey,' she said in a mildly annoyed tone. 'Let's get the cattle out.' She turned her horse and rode out to the cattle.

Four teenage girls stared after her in admiration.

From the corner of her eye, Jess saw Luke running towards the table, the last to come for breakfast. Feeling a sudden pang of weird shyness, she found something that needed tidying inside the trailer, but could still hear him asking, 'Any breakfast left?'

'There's some eggs and stuff in the pan,' said Rosie. 'Bread and tea are over there.'

There was a shuffle just outside and cutlery clinking. A cup was placed on the mudguard and Jess heard tea being poured.

'Asparagus!' she heard Luke laugh, as though he'd found something unexpected. 'Did Jess bring that?'

When Jess was sure he would have walked away she peered out the window. Luke had taken the whole pan and was sitting in a fold-out chair with it. His hair was wet and his clothes rumpled but fresh-ish. He looked up and saw her.

'Nice tips,' he called, waving an asparagus spear.

She bobbed back down, fighting a smile. By the time she emerged from the trailer, he was running back to the horses, the empty frying pan lying on the ground next to his empty chair.

Jess recognised Ryan as he rode towards the camp on a brown bay horse and raised his hat to Mrs Arnold. Through the dust that streaked his long narrow face, Jess could see his resemblance to Annie. 'Hey, Aunty Jude.'

'Hey,' said Mrs Arnold. 'Good to see you out here. You know Jess?'

Jess waved a hand. 'Hi.' She had heard so much about Ryan, about his drinking, his fights with Lawson, his horse-doping history, that she felt awkward suddenly saying hello to him.

Ryan looked at her as though he couldn't quite place her, but nodded a greeting.

'How've you been?' Mrs Arnold asked him.

'Yeah, getting my life together.'

'Got that demon back in the bottle?'

'Yeah,' he said sheepishly.

'Well, you make sure it stays there.'

Ryan turned to the girls. 'You brats gonna help count out the cattle?'

'I bags counting,' yelled Grace, taking off at a run towards the cattle.

Rosie, Shara and Jess took off after her.

'Is this fence switched on?' asked Rosie, slowing as they approached the white tape.

'No, Ryan switched it off,' said Grace, stopping to tie the lace on her runners.

'No, he—' began Jess.

But it was too late. Rosie grabbed for the tape to let herself through and shrieked as she was booted six feet across the ground, landing flat on her face alongside a particularly runny cowpat.

Grace collapsed to the ground with hysterical laughter, hands still fixed to her shoelace. 'You're as thick as a brick, Rosie!'

'I *hate* you, Grace Arnold!' Rosie screamed as she dragged herself off the ground. '*God*, I hate having a sister! *MU-U-UMMM!*' She began running after Grace, who had already taken off. 'I'm going to *kill* you!'

Still doubled up with laughter, Grace bolted for the last saddled horse. Shara ran after her. They both mounted the grey gelding and rode off double, Rosie screeching after them.

Jess watched with amusement as Lawson intercepted them and sent them straight back to the trailer. 'Stop spooking the cattle,' he roared at them. 'Get off that horse and take him back to Bob. We need him as a spare.'

Mrs Arnold walked out and took Grace by the collar, marching her to a stack of dirty dishes. Shara was ordered to help.

'Just dribble them out slowly,' Jess heard Lawson yelling to Luke and Stan as he rode back to the cattle. 'Keep those calves mothered up.'

Mrs Arnold sent Jess and Rosie to help Bob unhobble the spare horses and roll up the electric fencing. There were a dozen or so horses, some Jess recognised and some she didn't.

She was glad to see that Walkabout ran free. The filly recognised her instantly and nickered to her as she walked over. Jess pulled bread-crusts from her pocket and held them under the filly's snuffly nose. 'Hello, my friend,' she said, smiling and rubbing her forehead. 'Are you having a nice life, running around the outback?'

Walkabout was well over two years old now, ready to be started. As Jess scratched behind the filly's ears, she couldn't help wondering if she'd made the right decision years ago: to let Lawson buy Wally and wait for Marnie's foal. Then she thought of Dodger. There was no way she could have ever sold him to Bob to pay for Wally.

She gave Wally a quick rub and then, noticing that one of the ringers was watching, she moved on to the next horse. Marnie shuffled about in hobbles about twenty metres away and Jess headed in her direction. As she freed the mare's fetlocks, the ringer walked past and said, 'Nice mare, that one. Lawson's got a real good bunch of horses.' He touched the top of his hat. 'I'm Dave.'

'I'm Jess. I've got one of her foals, a chestnut filly.' Jess stood up and buckled the hobbles around Marnie's neck. 'I called her Opal, she's back at the homestead.'

'Oh yeah? I thought Lawson owned that one,' said

Dave, sounding only mildly interested.

Jess instantly bristled. 'No, she's mine. Lawson agreed to—' and before she knew it she was telling Dave the whole story of how she gave up Walkabout for Marnie's first foal.

Dave looked at Walkabout and then to Marnie. 'Either way, you're gonna get a nice horse. Opal's a good name too.'

'Lawson reckons opals are bad-luck stones,' said Jess.

'Nah, that's crap,' said Dave. 'That was made up by diamond traders when opals were first found in Australia. Our opals were such high quality they felt threatened by our trade.'

'Do you mine opals?'

'I do a bit of fossicking in my spare time.' Dave began telling her about his opal adventures, to the point of boring her.

Ryan rescued her. 'You coming, Dave?' he yelled as he rode towards them.

'On my way,' said Dave, slinging the reins over his horse's head.

'Hey, Jess,' said Ryan. 'Lindy asked if you could give Rosie a hand with the fences.'

Jess unhobbled the last horse and went to help Rosie. Together they rolled in what seemed like miles and miles of fencing tape, winding it around a big plastic reel. Rosie bitched and complained about Grace as they went. 'Mum just lets her get away with it. She never gets told off. I'm so sick of it . . .' They stored the rolls in the trailer and set about pulling out the pegs, carrying them back in armfuls to the camp.

A pile of rolled-up swags lay in a mountain by the trailer, along with pots, buckets, a motorbike, saddles and horse gear. Everything was packed into the trailer according to Mrs Arnold's instructions, and they took a last look around the site to check that they had everything packed up and the fire was out. Mrs Arnold slapped the side of the truck, and her husband closed the driver's side door and began hauling it all away.

12

'WE'VE GOT A few hours up our sleeves,' said Mrs Arnold as she plonked herself behind the wheel of the four-wheel drive. 'Let's go to the river and do the washing on our way to the next camp. Those men haven't done their washing in weeks.'

The girls peered inside the LandCruiser to see four large round bundles of clothes in nylon hay nets piled on the back seat.

'Stockies' jocks?' protested Grace. 'You gotta be *kidding* me!'

'You're not really going to make us *touch* those, are you?' Rosie said to her mother.

Mrs Arnold sighed, as though she had anticipated this argument. 'Get in.'

'Mu-um!' said Rosie, taking a few steps back. 'I am *not* getting in there. I'll be sick.'

'Ride on the running board then,' said Mrs Arnold, starting the engine.

'I bags the front seat,' said Grace, reaching for the doorhandle.

'I bags sitting on your lap,' said Shara, hopping in after her.

Jess took another look into the back seat. She could smell the clothes without even getting in. 'I think I'll ride on the running board too,' she said, stepping up and grabbing the roof racks.

Rosie folded her arms and stood her ground. 'It's because we're girls. Boys would never be made to do this!'

Mrs Arnold just shrugged, put the LandCruiser into gear and began to drive.

Rosie ever so slightly tilted her head in defiance.

Mrs Arnold rolled her eyes and braked. 'Are you coming?' she yelled back at her daughter.

Rosie didn't move.

Mrs Arnold looked thoughtful. 'If you come now, I won't make you wash *all* the undies.'

Rosie unfolded her arms and walked slowly, defiantly, to the car, making a point. She threw a cheeky look at her mother and reached for the roof racks. As she lifted a foot to the running rail, the four-wheel drive lurched away from her and Mrs Arnold drove off.

'MU-UM!' Rosie shrieked, infuriated.

Grace screamed with laughter. 'Suck eggs, Rosie,' she called out the window. Jess burst out laughing when she saw Rosie stamp her foot.

Mrs Arnold drove a wide loop around her daughter and then idled past her. 'Jump on,' she said out the window. Rosie ran to jump onto the running board, clutching the roof rack opposite Jess.

'Welcome aboard the BO Express!' Jess grinned at her.

Rosie scowled.

Jess enjoyed the wind and sun on her face as the car bumped a kilometre or so upriver to a spot that hadn't been messed up by the cattle.

At a clearing beside a waterhole, Mrs Arnold wrenched on the handbrake, and Grace and Shara tumbled out the front door, theatrically gasping for fresh air.

'I'm amazed *you* can smell anything, Grace,' snapped Rosie. 'You pong just as bad.' She walked to the back of the LandCruiser, opened the door and emerged with a long pair of barbecue tongs. 'I'm not touching anything grisly,' she said, 'and I'm not touching anything that's been worn by a ringer.'

'They do their own, don't worry,' said Mrs Arnold. 'Even I draw the line there.'

The girls cheered.

Under Mrs Arnold's instruction, they tied the string

hangers to the root of a tree and tossed three of the nets into the river, letting the current run through them. Mrs Arnold emptied the fourth net onto the sand. 'You can start on this bundle.' She pulled the more personal items out with the tongs and tossed them in a bucket of soapy water to soak.

'Why can't we just take them to a laundromat?' whined Rosie. 'This *is* the twenty-first century, you know.'

'Now where would be the fun in that?' said Mrs Arnold. 'I thought you wanted to go droving, not driving for hours to a laundromat.'

'Why don't the *boys* have to do any washing?' Grace grumbled and grudgingly picked out a shirt with her forefinger and thumb.

'Tom and Luke came last year and I'll have you know they did all the washing, *without* complaining,' said Mrs Arnold. 'You're the apprentices this year, so suck it up!'

The girls rubbed the clothes out and rinsed them in the warm river water, returning them to the nets and letting the gentle flow of the river do the final rinse.

As the day grew hotter, Jess realised the washing wasn't such a bad job, in the relative cool of the trees by the water. She squelched her bare toes in the grainy sand and imagined the spirits of ancient people tickling her feet. She could feel the earth alive with their songs. This strangely peaceful place had a heartbeat of its own, the river its lifeblood, the red earth its flesh. In the silvery mulga trees, pink and white corellas celebrated noisily as they feasted on the seeds, making music with the slow-moving water that dissipated into an echo of blue sky.

Mrs Arnold squatted next to Jess and gave her a rare smile. For a moment, her face looked as though it belonged to a different person.

'It's so beautiful out here,' Jess commented, rubbing a bar of soap over the leg of some jeans.

'Yes, it is,' agreed Mrs Arnold. 'It even makes *me* feel relaxed. Does a person good to get back out here and find their roots every now and then.'

'Are you from here?' asked Jess.

'Yeah, Harry and I grew up out here. I sold out my part of the property years ago. Didn't feel a need to own it in that way.'

'To Lindy's dad?'

'Yep, Harry's business partner.'

'So now Lindy is Lawson's business partner.'

'Yep.'

'Then how come she can tell him what to do?'

Mrs Arnold chuckled. 'I don't know, but he never argues with her. I'd love to know her secret.'

'So would I,' said Jess, almost to herself. 'Then I could get my filly back.' She looked at Mrs Arnold. 'Do you think Opal's going to come good? Have you ever seen a horse behave the same way as her?'

Mrs Arnold thought for a minute and then shook her head. 'No, I haven't. Something's definitely not right about her.'

'Bob reckons she's cursed,' said Jess.

'She's just a little filly with a sore head,' said Mrs Arnold.

'Lawson said she's got a bad temperament.'

'Wouldn't listen to Lawson. He says that about all Muscle's foals.'

'I'm scared he's going to take her from me too, like he did with Wally,' said Jess. 'Why does he have to make my life so hard? I hate him so much sometimes.'

'Lawson can seem a bit tough, but he's all right, Jess. There are better ways to get what you want than just getting cranky about things.'

There was a comfortable silence between them. Jess slapped the pair of jeans into the river and shook them about. Mrs Arnold grabbed a shirt from the dirty pile and swished it in the water, and they squatted side by side, rubbing and rinsing and squeezing.

Jess mulled over Mrs Arnold's words while she scrubbed, and soon the sounds and the smells of the mulga country eclipsed them and wrapped around her soul, making her feel completely at peace.

After a while Mrs Arnold sighed and said quietly, 'I miss you, brother.'

'I reckon I can hear Harry in the wind sometimes,' said Jess in almost a whisper. 'It just sounds so much like his wheezing.'

Mrs Arnold burst out laughing.

The serenity was shattered further when Grace threw a soggy pair of stocky's jocks at Rosie. Mrs Arnold hoisted up the legs of her jeans and waded through the creek towards her daughters. Her voice cut through the screeching of corellas.

As Jess watched, laughing at the circus that was the Arnold family, she pulled out her mobile phone to check for messages. When it stared blankly back at her, she shook it, then held it up to the sky. She turned about and repositioned herself but still there was no response. 'Oh my God, there's no reception out here!'

13

A HUGE MOB of cattle, flanked by men on horseback, ambled over a rise in the land. They were an awesome sight, with clouds of dust billowing behind them. The crack of the mens' stockwhips split the air, moving small mobs from the creek and onto the reserve where the pasture was thick and shade was plentiful. As the men backed off, the cattle lowered themselves to the ground with heavy groans and loud moos.

Luke rode into the lunch camp. He swung a leg over his horse and jumped down, then yanked at the girth and pulled the horse's gear off in one swift movement. Underneath it, Legsy was slick with sweat. He champed at his loose ring bit, blowing white froth over his chest. Luke led him to the old yellow ute and slung his reins over the bullbar.

Jess took a couple of buckets of water from the truck tanks and walked out to him.

'How's he going?' she asked as she slopped water over Legsy's back and gave the horse a rub under his girth area.

'He's loving all the work,' said Luke, taking a few steps to straighten out his legs. He tossed his saddle in the back of the ute, then unbuckled Legsy's bridle and swapped it for a halter. 'So you finally got yourself out here then?'

'Yeah.' She sponged more water onto the horse and moved towards his hind end.

'I knew you'd be coming out with Judy later.'

Jess stopped sponging. 'You *knew*?'

Luke smiled sheepishly.

She took her bucket and tossed the remaining water at him.

As Luke dived out of the way, the water splashed across his back and Legsy lurched sideways in surprise. 'Oi,' Luke laughed.

'You could have told me!'

'I was going to, but you got all . . .' He didn't finish, but put his hands on his hips, gave a hoity-toity wiggle and pulled a face.

'Yeah, maybe I did a bit,' admitted Jess, not quite ready to apologise yet.

'Hey, how cool is this ute?' he said, changing the subject and nodding towards the old paddock basher. 'It used to be Harry's. Lawson reckons it's been in the shed at the homestead for years. He changed the head gasket and got it going for this trip.'

Jess looked at the ute with its bald tyres, cracked windscreen, one door missing and rusty windscreen wipers. 'I could just imagine Harry driving around in that,' she laughed.

'It's an *HQ*,' said Luke. He still hadn't taken his eyes off it. 'They're such *beautiful* cars.'

'Each to their own, I s'pose,' mumbled Jess as she noticed a big rust hole on the front panel. 'Reckon it would tow a horse float?'

'Easy,' said Luke. He stepped closer to the ute and began running a hand along the length of its body. 'It's still got pretty straight panels. It'd probably spray up real nice.'

Bob appeared, leading three sweaty horses behind him. 'Nice ute, ay,' he called out as he walked past.

Luke ran after him, towing Legsy behind, and soon the pair of them were talking about 202 trimatics and cross-ply winter treads.

Jess rolled her eyes, moved to the next horse and held the other bucket of water up to its nose. Dave slung the horse's reins over the fence rail. 'Thanks, matey,' he said as he pulled some cigarettes out of his saddlebag. 'You not riding this muster?'

'Nah, not allowed,' said Jess. She pulled a face. '*Lawson's rules.*'

The stockman snorted and indicated his horse. 'Look after this bloke for me and you can ride him anytime. *Dave's rules!*' He winked and walked off, leaving the horse for her to unsaddle.

Jess lit up. 'Thanks,' she called after him, envisaging a ride to a hilltop to check her phone messages as soon as Mrs Arnold wasn't watching.

Dave joined Clarkey, who was sitting under a tree with his elbows on his knees, his hat on the ground. He unscrewed the cap off a bottle of water and began chugging it down, burping loudly when he finished.

As Jess unsaddled the horse, Ryan rode past. 'Can you guys come and give me a hand with the electric fence?' he called to the two men. 'The cattle are wandering onto private land, and the owner's going nuts at Lindy.'

Dave looked at his watch and then held up a freshly lit cigarette. 'Not my problem, matey, it's smoko time!'

'Clarkey?'

'They don't pay me enough to work on me lunchbreak,' the ringer answered. 'What *is* for lunch, anyway?'

Ryan waited a moment longer, and when neither of the men stood up, he turned his horse about, mumbling something under his breath as he rode away.

The girls spent the afternoon packing up the lunch

mess, loading the trailer again and relocating to the dinner camp. The new site was by a wide muddy river, flanked by stumpy mulga trees. Once there, they pegged the washing on makeshift clotheslines, set up cattle breaks and prepared a large pot of lamb stew, which they hung on an iron tripod over the campfire. Lindy had brought a side of lamb back to camp from her trip into town, which was a welcome change from the tinned meat the men had all been living on. Jess lifted the lid and stirred the chunks of her carrots and beans around with the potatoes and meat, poking them to see if they were soft.

'How's that foal? Any better yet?' asked Stanley Arnold as he stepped out of the trailer.

'The station's going to text me if she gets any worse. But I can't get any reception.' Jess frowned and patted the phone in her back pocket. 'I have to find a hill.'

Stan raised his eyebrows. 'You'll be lucky out here.'

'Hold up the lid to that pot,' said Mrs Arnold, joining Jess at the fire. As Jess did so, Mrs Arnold held a silver wine bladder over the pot and gave a long squirt of red liquid. 'That oughta liven it up a bit,' she said, peering into the pot and inhaling deeply. 'Don't mention that to Ryan and his mates, will you.'

'Promise,' said Jess, leaning over and sniffing. The stew smelled sensational.

Stanley sneaked up behind them and tried to stick

a finger in the pot, only to be smartly rapped over the knuckles with Mrs Arnold's spoon.

'Ouch! I was just gonna test it!' he cried, wringing his hand. 'See if it's fit for human consumption.'

'You can wait like the rest of them,' said Mrs Arnold. 'Why don't you do something useful while you're waiting, and collect some firewood? It's gonna be cold tonight.'

'Yeah, righto,' Stanley grumbled. 'Mean old woman.' He winked at Jess as he stalked off.

'If you find me some good hardwood, I'll knock up some treacle dumplings,' Mrs Arnold called after him.

Stanley's step lightened. 'Hardwood coming up!'

The sun disappeared over the horizon and the last traces of light faded quickly, until there was only the glow of the fire. With the day's bread already eaten, Mrs Arnold showed Jess how to make up a quick loaf of damper to go with the stew.

Jess was glad they'd had camp ready by nightfall. She was discovering that being a drover's cook was all about being organised. Tonight they were ahead on a few of their tasks and she was hoping to go for a night walk after all the dishes were washed and the dough was kneaded for tomorrow's bread. The moon was three-quarters full and would shed fantastic light. She had been thinking about Bob's words all afternoon.

That horse is from the min mins. She got debil debil *in her head.*

She approached Mrs Arnold, who was bringing the damper out of the ashes. 'Mrs Arnold?'

'Hmm? Here, grab a cloth and take hold of this.'

With the cloth full of damper, Jess asked, 'Can I go for a walk after dinner?'

'Go for a walk?' From the look on Mrs Arnold's face, Jess might as well have asked to go to Mars.

'Yes. I've just got some weird idea about looking for min min lights.'

'S'pose so, if you can get someone to go with you,' Mrs Arnold said doubtfully. 'Steer clear of the cattle, though.'

'Thanks, Mrs Arnold. I will.'

'I mean it, Jessica. Stay clear of the cattle, or they'll up and rush, you hear? If I find you anywhere near 'em, I'll brain you.'

Jess took her bowl of stew and joined the others around the fire. Lawson picked quietly at a guitar while Stanley spent the mealtime telling tall stories. He spun a yarn about a snake crawling into his sleeping bag, obviously designed to give the girls the creeps. Lindy just smiled, shook her head, and mopped up the last of her stew. Beyond them, Jess could see Luke and Bob under the bonnet of the old ute.

'Where's Dave?' asked Jess, with the vague idea of taking him up on his offer of his horse. A night ride would be even better than a night walk.

'He's on night watch with Ryan,' said Shara.

'Oh.' That dashed that idea. Jess got up and rinsed out her bowl. 'Who's coming for a night walk then?'

'Can we go tomorrow night?' said Rosie. 'I'm so tired.'

Jess looked to Grace, sure she would jump at the chance.

'I'm staying here,' Grace said, looking more than comfortable curled against her father, both their faces glowing warmly in the firelight. Jess turned to Shara with a questioning face.

'I'm with Rosie,' said Shara. 'I haven't slept properly for two nights.'

Jess's shoulders slumped. 'But I'm not allowed to go by myself,' she complained.

'I'll come,' said Luke, appearing on the other side of the fire, covered in grease. He picked the lid off the stew pot and looked around for a bowl. 'After a quick feed, anyway. Jeez, that smells all right.'

Jess grinned.

A dark look came over Mrs Arnold's face. 'Sit yourself down, Luke,' she said. 'I'm responsible for the girls while they're out here, and I'm not letting 'em go walkabout with some grubby ringer in the middle of the night.' She raised an eyebrow, daring him to challenge her.

Luke found a bowl and a ladle, then turned to Mrs Arnold with one in either hand. He smiled his most charming of smiles. 'It's okay, Mrs A. She'll be in good hands.'

'Yeah, that's exactly what I'm worried about,' Mrs Arnold said in a slow, menacing voice. 'Now get some dinner and sit down.'

A ripple of giggles went through the camp.

14

JESS SQUIRMED in her swag. She pushed Grace's knee away from her ribs and curled up in a ball to stop her bladder from aching. On the other side of her, Rosie snored loudly. Outside the window, Jess could hear the truck's CD player crackling with country music. She pulled the sleeping bag up over her freezing nose.

In the end, her bladder got the better of her and she wriggled out of her swag. As she lowered herself to the floor of the truck, Mrs Arnold's hand reached out and wrapped around her ankle.

'I'm busting for a whiz.'

'Well, come straight back.'

Jess pulled on a jacket and slipped out the narrow door. In the soft orange light of the campfire, she could make out two people lying T-boned, one with their head on the other's belly. Lawson and Lindy.

No wonder he does what he's told! Wait till I tell the others!

'I'm gonna tell them both to finish up,' Lindy was murmuring to Lawson. 'We've got enough riders now that the girls are here. Gracie's pretty handy on cattle.'

Lawson shrugged. 'You're the boss.'

Jess stopped in her tracks, unsure if she had heard right. She still couldn't believe that Lawson would bow to anyone. She shook her head and kept creeping, barefoot, towards the riverbank. She squatted under a tree, and looked up to the stars that twinkled through its canopy.

As she stood and made her way back to the camp, a twig cracked behind her. She spun around. 'Dave!'

'Hey,' he whispered, stumbling through the bushes towards her.

Jess wrapped her jacket tightly around her. 'Aren't you watching the cattle?' she said, cautiously.

'Yep,' he said. 'They're not doing much, sleeping and farting mostly.' He stepped closer. 'Saw you trotting across the camp and thought I'd come and offer you a drink.' He held up the crumpled silver remains of Mrs Arnold's not-so-secret stash and gave it a shake. 'Hmm, I seem to have emptied that, but I do have a couple of cans of rumbo left,' he said, tossing the empty bladder over his shoulder and pulling the cans out of his pockets.

'No thanks,' Jess said politely, looking around for a way out of there that didn't involve brushing past him.

'Don'tcha drink?' he said, sounding alarmed.

'No.'

'Just have a little one,' he insisted, holding the can out to her.

'No thanks,' she said, pushing it away.

'Ah, c'mahhn, don'tcha know how to have fun?'

'I have to go back to the truck, Dave. Mrs Arnold is sitting up waiting for me.'

But Dave didn't give up. 'I need a drinking buddy, it's so bloody dry around here!' He took another step towards her, and she noticed he was unsteady on his feet. 'I only wanna *talk*. I don't bite!'

Jess leaned away from him. 'Talk about what?

'What's a young thing like you doing out here?' He held up the cans and pulled a comical face. 'And not having any fun?'

'Well, you know what Mrs Arnold's like – the word "fun" doesn't seem to be in her vocabulary. In fact, she'll probably blow a gasket if I'm not back in that trailer soon.' Jess faked a laugh as she pushed past him.

Dave held out an arm and wrapped it around her waist. 'You didn't answer my question,' he said, suddenly sounding nasty. 'I asked you what you're doing out here. No bloody place for a bunch of girls, if you ask me.'

'Hey!' Jess jumped backwards and shoved his hand away. 'We've got every right to be here. Those were Harry Blake's cattle, and he was family to us.' She tried to dodge past again, but he stepped sideways to block her.

'Let me past!'

'Leave her alone, Dave.'

Jess looked past Dave and saw Luke walking into the cover of the trees.

Dave spun around and gave a mocking laugh. 'You wait your turn, boy.'

Luke put a hand on Dave's shoulder. 'I said, get away from her.'

Dave took a step forward and put his face close to Luke's. 'Why don't you find your own drinking buddy?' he growled.

'Why don't you sober up?' Luke shoved him hard in the chest, and as Dave lurched backwards, Luke shoved him again.

Dave staggered a few drunken steps before finding his feet, then lunged back, swinging a fist at Luke.

Luke ducked easily and hammered a fist straight into the man's face. It connected with a sickening crunch, and Jess gasped as she watched Dave reel backwards and roll about with his hands over his face. He unleashed a tirade of abuse at both Luke and Jess before collapsing in a silent heap.

Luke bent to pick up the cans that Dave had dropped and, one by one, emptied their contents onto the ground. 'You okay?' he asked.

She nodded and shivered. 'Are you just gonna leave him there?'

Luke gave a short, scornful laugh. 'I can give him another one and roll him into the river if you want.'

She shook her head quickly.

They both stepped back as Dave pulled himself off the ground. 'I'll give *you* another one,' he snarled.

Luke dropped the cans and stepped towards him.

Dave took a moment to get steady on his feet, then sized Luke up, who stood as solid as a rock, looking down at him. 'You'll keep,' Dave muttered, and to Jess's relief, he stumbled away, wiping his face with his sleeve and spitting on the ground.

Luke turned to her. 'You sure you're okay?'

She nodded. 'How'd you know I was down here?'

'The dogs whined when you walked past, then I saw him follow. I can spot a drunk a mile off.'

Jess watched Dave disappear along the river. 'I thought he was a nice guy,' she said, willing herself not to cry.

'Probably is when he's sober,' said Luke. His voice changed. 'Need a hug?'

She looked at him and nodded, and he came closer and wrapped both arms around her. Jess put her face into his chest and could hear his heart thumping. He held her stiffly for a while, with his chin on her head, and then she heard him begin to breathe more easily. 'You're not used to seeing stuff like that, are you?' he asked quietly.

She looked up at him. 'No, that freaked me out a bit.'

'Sorry,' he whispered.

'No, *I'm* sorry,' she said, 'for being such a cow to you at Harry's place. I was horrible.'

He gave her a squeeze. 'No biggy.'

She squeezed him back and put her freezing nose into the warmth of his neck. She drank in his smell – no soap or washing powder, just him: clean, fresh, but mixed with the muskiness of horse and woodsmoke. Then she startled. 'Oh no! Mrs Arnold! She'll come looking for me,' she whispered urgently, pulling away. 'She'll kill us both!'

'Wait,' said Luke, grabbing her hand. 'Aren't you going to tell her what happened?'

Jess groaned. 'I'll get sent home. And what if Dave tries to have you up for assault?' She looked at Luke pleadingly. 'Please don't tell anyone.'

'Are you nuts?' said Luke. 'He was *drunk*!'

'I think Lindy is going to sack them anyway. I overheard her talking to Lawson.'

'Dave was harassing you.'

'He didn't hurt me. I'll be fine. I'd better hurry before Mrs Arnold comes looking for me.' Jess began to pull away. 'If she finds me down here with you, I really will get sent home.'

But Luke kept hold of her hand. He pulled her back into his arms. 'Are you sure you're okay?'

'Yes.'

He swept her hair off her face and looked down at her with a calm intensity. 'You tell me if he comes anywhere near you again.'

'Okay,' she said, feeling suddenly self-conscious.

'If he even looks at you.'

She nodded. 'Um, I have to go.' She pulled herself away from him and felt her hand slip from his, then tiptoed hurriedly across the camp to the trailer.

Later, lying in her swag, Jess couldn't sleep, unable to stop reliving the sense of Luke's warm arms wrapped around her and the way he had looked at her. Maybe Rosie was right?

She pulled the curtain back and looked out the window. Only a flat pile of embers remained of the campfire, where Lawson and Lindy sat quietly. The generator hummed and music still crackled softly from the cabin of the truck. After what seemed like hours, she drifted into a fitful sleep.

15

SHE WOKE TO her foot being violently shaken.

'Time to get up,' said Mrs Arnold.

Jess groaned, stretched and looked out the window at the pink and orange sunrise. The campfire had died and there were two empty cups, upended, where Lawson and Lindy had been.

Suddenly, Bob ran into the camp waving and gesturing madly. Jess noticed he held Mrs Arnold's empty wine bladder in one hand.

'Something's happened to Bob!' said Jess, loud enough to wake the others up.

Shara, with her hair sticking up and eyes half-open, grunted and shuffled up next to her. 'What's going on?'

Outside, Lindy appeared from the cabin of the truck, hopping about and pulling on her boots. She listened briefly to Bob before sticking two fingers in her mouth and issuing a sharp whistle.

Grace instantly sat up and crawled to the tiny window. 'Let me see,' she said, squeezing between Jess and Shara.

The entire camp erupted into chaos.

Lawson emerged shirtless from somewhere and was bellowing at Ryan within seconds. 'I told you to keep an eye on those drinking buddies of yours,' he roared. 'There was to be no alcohol on this trip!'

Ryan, looking drowsy and wearing only a pair of shorts, held up his hands in puzzlement. 'I didn't know there was any!'

'Uh-oh,' Jess heard Mrs Arnold mumble.

Lawson clenched his fists and raised them at Ryan, as though he wanted to punch him from one end of the camp to another.

'*I* wasn't drinking!' Ryan protested. 'I'm sober as a judge!'

Lawson dropped his fists and stormed off, calling for Stanley. He wrenched open the door of the truck and snatched his shirt from the front seat.

Lindy ran towards the trailer. 'We got some stolen horses, Jude. Could you come and give us a hand?'

'Sure they didn't just get loose?' asked Mrs Arnold, reaching for her jacket.

'Someone's unbuckled the hobbles and left them behind.'

'Which horses are missing?'

'Marnie and Walkabout.'

Jess shot upright and smacked her head on the ceiling of the trailer. 'Ouch!'

'Grab some halters, girls.' said Mrs Arnold as she disappeared out the door.

The trailer came alive as four girls scrambled for four pairs of boots that all looked the same. One by one they filed out of the door and grabbed halters and buckets, anything to help lure a wayward horse.

Luke ran into the camp, yelling, 'The cattle are out – someone pulled the fencing down!'

Lawson swore and turned to Mrs Arnold. 'We've got some cattle to muster too, Jude.'

'Oh, so *now* you want us to ride?' said Grace, as she stepped out of the trailer.

'Who said anything about you riding?' Lawson said, shortly.

Grace stopped in her tracks and put her hands on her hips, a look of fury on her face. Lindy roared up on a motorbike and indicated to the seat behind her. 'Hop on!'

Grace hoisted a leg over the back of the bike and planted herself behind Lindy. She pulled a face at Lawson as they buzzed off into the breaking day.

Jess ran straight to Bob, who was hurriedly pulling saddles out of the tack box. 'How long have the horses been missing?'

'Not even an hour, ay. I checked on 'em before I went for a wash down the creek.' He gave her a reassuring look. 'Can't have gone far. We'll get 'em back.' He slung a couple of bridles over his shoulder and raced off.

Jess ran back to the trailer and hastily pulled a jacket on, buttoning it up to her chin. Then she rummaged around in Mrs Arnold's cooking gear, grabbed a rolling pin, shoved it down the front of her jacket and set off at a run. She had no idea what she would do with it, but she certainly wasn't going to let Wally fall into the hands of those men.

Way ahead she could see the dust trail of the motorbike and hear Lindy shouting. As Jess jogged in its wake, hoofbeats rang out behind her and she turned to see a jet black horse approaching her.

Luke cantered up on Legsy and held out an arm. Needing no further invitation, she took hold of his elbow and vaulted up as he slowed beside her.

'They've stolen Walkabout,' she said, planting herself firmly behind the saddle.

'Yeah, I know. Lawson's ropeable.' Luke turned the horse and cantered after Lindy and Lawson.

'They must've let the cattle out on purpose so they could get away with the horses,' said Jess.

'Yeah, probably.'

'Walkabout doesn't have any brands! They'll be able

to mark her themselves and put her through the sales.'

Lawson cantered up on Slinger. He ground the horse to a halt and swung him around. 'The cattle are all headed for the creek,' he said. 'It'll be chaos if they all jump in together.'

'Want us to go head them off?' asked Luke.

'Lindy and Stan have already headed out clockwise. I'm going to circle in the other direction and head them off. You guys ride to the next bore and make sure there's water in the trough; if we can head the cattle back there before they get too thirsty, they might leave the river alone. Fill the troughs up nice and full and open any gates for them.'

'Yep,' said Luke.

Lawson paused and looked at Jess. 'And then *I'll* be going for that filly, Jessica.'

Jess scowled and looked away. She heard him click up his horse and gallop away.

Luke turned Legsy and they cantered off in the direction of the bore.

'Dave knew that Wally and Marnie were my favourite horses,' said Jess. 'I told him all about Opal too. He's done this out of spite.'

'And you thought he was a nice guy.'

'He better not take it out on the horses. He better not—' She didn't even want to think about it.

They cantered steadily along the wide dirt track before coming to a wire gate strung across the road. Jess slid off the back of the colt, slipped a wire loop off the gatepost, then dragged it, clanging and jingling, back to the fenceline. With the track opened for the cattle, they set out to look for the bore.

After loping for quite a distance, the colt grew tired and slowed to a walk. Luke and Jess rode in silence, awed by the sense of limitless space that radiated around them. Jess rested her head against Luke's back and wrapped her arms around his waist. As Legsy lunged over a clump of grass, she lurched into his shoulder blades.

'Ouch, what was that?' he asked.

'A rolling pin.'

He laughed. 'You're so funny, Jess.'

'And I'm not afraid to use it,' she said, readjusting the rolling pin and replacing her hands on his ribs. His torso was lean and sinewy, but beneath his shirt, the bones down his right side felt all wrong. She had noticed them before but had never asked. 'Did you break a rib or something?'

'Five of them.'

'How?' She felt his chest lift and fall as he drew a deep breath, and she suddenly felt awkward. 'Did a drunk do that to you?'

'Yeah. Long time ago,' said Luke.

Jess was so shocked she couldn't think of what to say. She ran her hands over his ribcage, wishing she could smooth them out and make that part of his history go away.

He put his hand on hers and moved it away. 'I don't even think about that stuff when I'm out here, Jess.'

'What do you think about?'

'When I'm out here alone with the cattle I just look around and soak it all in. There's no sense of time. It's really hard to explain.'

Jess looked around her. Out to their left, jagged rocks rose magnificently from the horizon like giant sleeping dinosaurs. A creature, timid and unseen, rustled in a shrub as they rode past. 'It's a really spiritual place,' Jess murmured, hoping she didn't sound too kooky.

'Yeah, it is.'

'I keep thinking I'm going to find answers in the land, like Harry used to say. I can't stop thinking about Opal being a min min horse.'

'Bob calls her the *debil debil* horse,' Luke laughed. 'But I think he's only joking.'

'Reckon she could be cursed? I have nightmares about her, sometimes.'

Luke took a while to answer. 'Did you know that there were tribes of people in ancient Britain who had horses and wolves as their totems?'

'No.'

'Maybe you have horse dreaming.'

Jess thought of Filth and Fang and their desperate loyalty to Luke. 'I think you definitely have wolf dreaming.'

'Yeah, those dumb dogs. They appeared out of nowhere. I swear to God, it was as if they just chose me and I had no say in it.'

'I feel like that with Opal.'

'Maybe you have Opal dreaming.' He pointed ahead. 'There's the turkey's nest,' he said, pointing to a big earthen dam, rising up out of the flat country. A rusty windmill stood motionless beside it, despite the gentle breeze. 'Hope it's got some water in it.'

Jess noticed a shadow slink behind the base of the dam. She felt Luke stiffen. He had seen it too.

'What was that?' she hissed, squinting into the harsh morning sun.

Another shadow slunk between the windmill and the dam.

'There's another one. It was a person!' Jess whispered urgently. 'There are two of them.'

Luke gathered Legsy's reins and slowed his walk. 'You still got that rolling pin?'

'Let's just turn around and go back,' she said. 'It's not worth it.'

'It's too late, they've seen us. Give me the rolling pin.'

'Let's just go, Luke. I want to go back. You're scaring me.'

Luke drew the horse to a halt and turned in the saddle. 'Don't be frightened. I won't let them hurt you, Jess.' He reached into her jacket and pulled out the rolling pin.

'I know, that's what scares me.' She reached her arm through to the reins and grabbed one. 'Luke, I want to go back,' she pleaded.

All of a sudden, Luke burst out laughing. 'It's a little calf! Two little calves; look at them!'

Jess exhaled a huge billowing breath of relief. 'That scared the life out of me!'

Luke chuckled as he dismounted Legsy and led him closer to the bore. 'Poor little fellas are just looking for a drink. The dam's fenced off.'

Jess slipped off Legsy's rump and walked alongside him. 'Any water in the trough?'

Luke walked a few more metres before answering. 'Nope!' He looked up. 'There's something stuck in the wind-wheel.'

'Gross, it's a bird,' said Jess, noticing the lump had feathers. 'God, it's huge, what is it? Do they get pelicans around here?'

'Whatever it is, it must have been pretty dumb to fly into a windmill.'

'Maybe it had heatstroke,' Jess shrugged.

'Birds don't get heatstroke.'

'It's possible!' she said, indignantly. 'Global warming and all that!'

'Oh, shut up,' said Luke.

'Hey, maybe it flew over from the Northern Territory because it was melting!'

'Yeah, yeah, very funny.' Luke took hold of the rusty metal frame of the windmill and prepared to climb. 'Either way, I'll have to go up there and get it out.' He was about to start hauling himself up when Jess saw his eye catch on something in the distance. She looked behind her in the same direction.

A spiral of dust was twisting out of the ground, sucking leaves and powdery red earth up into its vortex, and gliding over the ground towards them.

'A willy-willy,' said Luke. 'Turn your back to it, Jess!'

Jess turned and shielded her eyes from its dust as it whirled into her, grabbing at her clothes and messing up her hair, before dissipating quite suddenly into stillness and fading out.

Where the willy-willy had cleared a path along the ground, a twinkling caught Jess's eye. She bent and brushed away the dirt. A small piece of rock lay in the dry sand, craggy and grey.

'It's an opal!' Jess picked it up and turned it over in the

palm of her hand. Where it had broken open, the rough exterior encased a solid centre of red and turquoise, green and gold. It was the most beautiful thing she had ever seen. 'Just like Dave talked about.'

'See,' said Luke. 'You do have opal dreaming.'

'Don't be silly,' said Jess. 'Maybe it's a floater. Usually you have to go digging for opals, but every now and then a chunk comes to the surface.' She rolled it in her hand, fascinated by it.

'Weird stuff always happens around you,' said Luke.

'Opal,' said Jess, almost to herself. 'It's like I've found a little piece of her spirit.' She carefully placed the stone into her jeans pocket. 'Hey – can I borrow Legsy, while you deal with the dodo bird?'

16

'REMEMBER, LEGSY'S a stallion now,' said Luke, as he gave her a leg up. 'Don't let go of him or you'll never see him again. I don't want him running off to join the brumbies.'

'Are there brumbies around here?'

'No, but you know what I mean.'

'I promise I'll be careful with him,' said Jess, adjusting the stirrups. 'I just want to go for a bit of a ride – see if the land has anything else to show me.'

'Don't go too far. You haven't got any water.'

'Legsy'll look after me, won't you, boy?' She gave the stallion a pat. 'See you in about an hour.'

As Jess set out across an open stretch of patchy grasslands, she pulled her phone from her jacket pocket, switched it on, then she tucked it back into her pocket. She legged the stallion from side to side and he responded lightly to her touch. 'Hmm, nice,' she commented, and made her way to a small, open grove of stumpy mulga shrubs, sparsely dotted over the reddish earth. They had the bluntly cut ends and fuzzy new growth of trees that had been harvested.

As Jess rode into the grove, the scenery became identical all around; with nothing to distinguish the way home, it was almost like being in a maze. The sun was getting higher and she made note of the shadows stretching from the western side of the shrubs. She reached out and snapped small branches from the taller of the trees to mark her way.

Legsy walked with big ground-covering strides, brushing his legs through the silvery grey perennials that grew out of the dry land. Jess let him have his head and settled into the rhythm of his gait. 'They don't call you Legsy for nothing,' she said, as she patted his neck and watched the ground roll along beneath, alert for anything shiny or out of the ordinary. It would be cool to find another opal. She passed an old car tyre, the occasional crushed beer can and a dead snake – nothing remarkable.

As she drew further away from the bore, the occasional ironbark tree popped up and the trees became taller. She followed a cattle trail up and over a small rocky hill. When she got to the top, she stopped and pulled out her phone – still no reception.

She rode on, coming down the other side; the trees

suddenly opened onto a vast stretch of knee-high pasture. Legsy snatched at mouthfuls of grass as he walked through it, taking advantage of the long rein Jess gave him. She took a deep breath as a small breeze cooled her face, rippling the grass gently in its wake.

Legsy startled suddenly. 'Whoa!' Taken off-guard, Jess grabbed at the pommel of the saddle. The stallion came to an abrupt halt, snorting suspiciously, his legs set wide apart.

'What is it, Legs?' she said, quickly gathering the reins. She held onto his head as he began to turn in nervous circles.

Jess pulled him back around and tried to kick him up, but he only shuffled backwards. She kicked him again, but he jumped sideways in a big frightened leap, snorting loud blasts of snot into the air.

'Easy, boy,' she soothed, wondering if she should take warning and head back. 'What is it?'

She scanned the countryside, hoping it wasn't a black snake – or worse, a disgruntled ringer. Instead, she saw a small brown lump move through the long grass. 'It's a goat, you big sook!' Then she saw several more. 'Haven't you ever seen one before?'

She let him stop and have a look. His whole body had gone as hard as a rock, and he held his head high, ears jutting forward. One front leg trembled slightly. Jess patted him on the neck and he jumped out of his skin again, making her laugh. 'Hey, you big baby!'

After several minutes of letting the stallion become acquainted with a new species, Jess managed to coerce him to tiptoe gingerly through the herd, sidestepping with alarm and snorting mistrustfully each time a goat lifted its head and bleated at him.

Safely through the goat herd, the stallion lengthened his stride and relaxed into a brisk walk again, through more small hills and narrow winding trails. She let him have his head for a while and marvelled at the intense blue of the sky and the clarity of colour all around her. It was as though someone had cleaned the air with Windex. Then Legsy shortened his stride again and lifted his head.

'More goats?' said Jess, bunching up the reins. 'Just about time to turn back anyway.' Before turning him about, she pulled out her phone and double-checked for any reception. 'Useless thing.'

Legsy sniffed the air again and began bouncing on his hocks. He arched his neck and a deep throaty rumble came from his chest.

'You like goats now?' Jess murmured, stuffing her phone back into her top pocket and taking her reins in two hands.

Legsy nickered again and began prancing. His back rolled to and fro beneath her. 'Who are you showing off to, fella?' she said, running a hand down the length of his mane. As the words left her mouth she heard a distant whinny.

Legsy immediately picked up his stride and began roaring and bellowing. Jess held him tight. 'Oh, great. A mob of mares.'

And then she caught a glimpse of movement in a thicket of sandalwood trees some distance away, a red and white rump, jumping about but not getting anywhere. 'Wally?' Her heart stopped momentarily. '*Wally!*'

Jess knew that snow-capped rump anywhere. She pushed Legsy into a trot and struggled to hold him steady as he began cantering on the spot. 'Whoa, big fella,' she said soothingly, fighting for control. She struggled to get a better look through the trees.

As she managed to coerce Legsy closer to the thicket, she saw that Walkabout was tied to a tree. The filly was pulling against it with all her might, twisting and shaking her head. Behind her, Jess could just make out a large flat thing – then she heard a familiar sound: horse hooves banging on a tail ramp. 'Oh my God!' she whispered, still fighting to hold the stallion steady. 'They're gonna put her on a truck!'

Jess squinted as a man came into sight, and she recognised Clarkey's black hat and scrawny frame. The air split in two with the sound of a stock whip as it lashed over Wally's rump. Jess jumped as though she herself had been whipped, sending Legsy into yet another tailspin. She pulled him around to see the filly lurch forward and smash her shoulder into a tree. Legsy screamed loudly and Clarkey wandered out from the thicket.

He saw her. For a split second, Jess's eyes connected with his.

In a blind panic, she turned the stallion and booted him. 'Get up, Legs!' she clucked madly. '*Hah! Go!*'

The stallion leapt into a gallop and Jess steered him straight back to the hills. She rode flat chat, ducking the low tree branches, barely managing to steer Legsy along the small windy track, up and over the hill. Her feet jolted into her stirrup irons as he propped down the other side. Then, as they reached the open pasture a small white goat popped up its head and bleated.

Legsy saw it before Jess did, and reacted with lightning-fast reflexes. In a single, terrified sideways leap, he collided with a tree, crushing her leg and smacking her head into a low branch. As Legsy rebounded off its trunk she tumbled from the saddle, landing shoulder-first on a pile of rocks.

The last thing Jess heard before drifting into a haze was the rumble of Legsy's hooves, retreating into the distance.

17

THE HOT AFTERNOON SUN blazed on Jess's face, burning into her eyelids and forcing them to open. A buzzing sound went around and around in her head. She licked her dry cracked lips and tried to generate some moisture in her mouth.

'My leg,' she moaned, reaching down and finding her jeans torn. The leg beneath was grazed and sticky with blood. Flies crawled over it and she waved them off.

A twig snapped near where she lay in the dust and she froze. Then a horse snorted softly down the back of her neck. 'Legsy?' She twisted her head around. '*Wally!*'

Jess scrambled to her feet and looked around for the ringers, her eyes darting from tree to rock to shrub. Wally stepped back out of her way. All Jess could see were short, stumpy mulga trees. The sun beat down, casting shadows directly beneath them and giving no clue as to east or west. There were no sounds apart from the tweeting of birds and the rustle of leaves in the breeze. A long way away, a cow mooed.

'Wally,' Jess said gently. The little horse hung her haltered head, a broken rope dangling between her front legs. Her flanks were sunken with thirst and she was in a lather of sweat. 'Oh my God, Wally! What have they done to you?' Jess stumbled as she went to the filly's side. 'Whoa, I feel woozy.'

When she managed to get her balance, Jess ran her hands over Walkabout, inspecting every inch of her for injuries. The horse had large welts on either side of her rump and rope marks around her hocks. 'They tried to get you onto that truck, didn't they?' Jess said, rubbing Wally's neck. 'You're a good, brave girl for not going on.' She unbuckled the halter, which was too small for the horse and squeezed tightly. Jess threw it on the ground in disgust and rubbed at the cruel marks that ran around the filly's nose.

Then a terrible realisation hit her. 'Oh no, Wal, *where's Legsy*?'

She scanned all around her again. Beyond the mulgas were tall, jagged rocks and tussocks of grass sprouting from the parched land.

'And *Marnie*. Is Marnie with you?' Jess's heart sank as she failed to sight the mare. 'Where are the horses?' she moaned, walking directionless into nowhere. Her leg hurt and her head pounded. 'Oh, Wally. What have I done?'

When she couldn't spot a single landmark she recognised to give her a clue to the direction of the bore, she stopped and looked back to Wally. 'Which way do I go, Wal? I have to find them!'

Walkabout stood motionless, her ears following Jess's every move.

Jess took hold of her mane. 'Easy, Wally,' she said. 'I need some help, little one.' Facing the filly's tail, Jess took one step forward and threw her leg up and over the filly's back, landing as softly as she could. Wally's skin quivered and Jess ran a hand quietly down her neck. 'You know where they are, don't you?'

Walkabout took a few tentative steps, then stopped. Jess stayed quiet for a moment and let the young horse continue at her own pace until she stretched her legs into a relaxed walk, away from the rocks. 'That's it,' said Jess. 'You lead, little buddy. Find Legsy.'

Jess sat passively on Wally's back, letting the filly find her own way. Her head pounded and her skin felt as though it was shrinking in the intense heat. The rocking sensation of Wally's gait began to make her feel woozy and she held onto the filly's mane to steady herself. As long as she could stay on Wally's back, she was sure the filly would lead her to the camp.

It felt like hours before Jess heard the crack of stockwhips and saw the army of red cattle marching through its own dust. Through the dust cloud she could make out Lawson and Stanley on their flanks, heading them towards the bore.

She cupped her hands over her mouth. 'Coo-ee!'

Both men immediately looked up. Lawson launched Slinger into a canter and headed her way.

'Jessica! Where've you been? There are people out looking everywhere. Legsy came thundering back without you. Luke's out of his head, he's galloping around everywhere trying to find—' He stopped, spotting her torn jeans. 'Are you hurt?'

'Oh, thank God you found Legsy,' Jess said in a wave of relief, then shook her head, making it throb even worse. 'I'm just thirsty.'

Lawson dismounted, pulled a water canteen from his saddlebag and handed it to her. 'Where'd you find Wal?'

Jess guzzled the warm plastic-tasting water, blissfully wet against her parched throat, and imagined it flowing straight to her brain cells, plumping them up and re-hydrating them. She wiped her mouth. 'She found me.'

'I see you broke her in for me,' he said, sounding unimpressed.

Jess bristled. 'I started her ages ago. Like you promised

I could,' she reminded him, then muttered. 'Don't bother thanking me.' She finished off the last of the water.

'She okay?' Lawson ran a hand over Wally and found the welts on her rump. 'What the— Who's been flogging her?'

'Clarkey. I found her tied to a tree—' She paused, the words stuck in her throat. 'They had a truck.'

'Did you see Marnie?' he demanded.

'No. But I heard a horse going up the truck ramp.'

The anguish that flashed across Lawson's face took Jess by surprise. He looked a nanosecond from bursting into tears.

How does it feel? she felt like saying.

Lawson quickly pulled himself together and cursed instead, as any heartache became boiling anger.

'My best horse, *again*,' he said. 'I'm going to tear Ryan apart limb by limb if she's not found!'

'Why is it *his* fault?'

'They were *his* drunken mates,' Lawson yelled. 'He promised me faithfully there'd be no problems.'

'Don't yell at *me*!' said Jess, her head pounding.

Lawson cursed again. 'It was Harry's dying wish that I forgive Ryan, and look what's happened. He hasn't changed at all!' He stabbed a finger at her. 'Always trust your gut, Jess. Don't do anything that you know is wrong just to please other people.'

'I trusted my gut with you,' she said, listening impassively to his ranting. 'And you took my filly off me again. You're no better than your brother.' She turned to walk away.

'How dare you compare me with that drunk?' he called after her. 'I put Marnie out of work for nearly a year to give you that foal, I'll have you know. Your filly is in good hands – the best of hands!' He began stomping after her. 'If I'd left it to you, she'd be bloody dead by now and you'd be two hundred bucks out of pocket!'

'You told everyone that she was your filly!' she yelled back at him.

'She still is,' he thundered.

'She's *mine*!' Jess screamed. 'The day she was weaned, she became *my* horse. You had no right to just take her without asking me first.'

'I had every right! Jesus, Jessica, when are you going to stop arguing with me at every chance you get and trust me?'

'I gave you my trust when I let you buy Wally. I gave you my trust when you said I could buy Opal. You *blew* my trust when you took her away from me!'

Lawson paused and pulled himself together. He lowered his voice to a cool icy tone. 'Opal's at the homestead and the staff are on strict instructions to message me as soon as anything happens with her.' He pulled his phone out of his top pocket and shook it at her. 'I'll hear as soon as her condition changes.'

'No, you won't, because I told them to ring *me* if anything happened,' she said, ripping her phone out of her top pocket and shaking it back at him.

'What, on that thing? You didn't, did you?' Lawson shook his head and laughed in disbelief. 'Tell me you didn't do that!'

Jess shrugged at him.

'Jessica, this is a *satellite* phone. It's the only sort that'll work out here. You won't get any messages on your thing.'

Jess stared at his phone, and a cold sickly feeling rushed over her.

'Good one, Jess. Now we don't know if Opal's alive or dead.'

At that moment, Bob appeared on foot, his jeans rolled up to mid-calf and two knobbly black feet poking out below. 'I'll take you back to camp if you want, Jess.' She could see him looking her up and down from behind his wraparound sunnies and big hat. 'You're not lookin' too good, ay?'

Lawson hoisted himself back onto his horse and kicked it. As he rode away, he yelled over his shoulder, '*And he's not my brother!*'

As Jess watched him gallop back to the cattle, she put

her hands over her face and burst into tears, sinking to the ground.

Bob squatted next to her. 'Hey, come on now, missy. It'll be okay.'

'No, it won't,' Jess sobbed. 'It's my fault the ringers stole Lawson's good horse. Everything's my fault.'

'Nah, them ringers are no good,' said Bob. 'Bunch of alcos; it's not your fault.'

'I've probably gone and got Opal killed too. I didn't know Lawson had a satellite phone. I didn't know you even *needed* a satellite phone.'

Bob didn't respond to that one. Jess began sobbing even harder.

Eventually Bob stood and ran a hand over Walkabout's shoulder. 'C'mon, let's take this filly back. Give her a drink and some feed.' He reached for his belt to use as a rope. 'Coming?'

18

JESS FOUND THAT the more she walked, the more her leg seemed to loosen up and stop aching, but the fabric of her jeans rubbed against the grazed skin. She stopped, rolled up her jeans leg, then kept walking. Walkabout grazed and dawdled behind her. As they drew further away from the cattle, the land fell silent around them. The only sounds were their legs brushing through the Mitchell grass and birdcalls from distant skies.

Jess and Bob had been walking at a casual pace for a little over an hour when Bob stopped and squatted beside a flat rock almost hidden beneath the tufty grass. He brushed away the dead leaves and soil and ran his fingers around some rings that were engraved in the rock. They looked just like the ripples on a waterhole when a pebble is thrown into it.

'How did you know that was there?' Jess asked.

'Those stones showed me.' Bob turned and pointed to

a few unremarkable rocks she had just walked past. 'That's a cairn, it points us to the trees, telling us which way, and the carving tells us that it's water. The signs are here for everybody if they know what to look for.'

On a second look, Jess noticed that the rocks looked carefully arranged.

Bob ran his hand along the underside of the pile. 'See how the rock beneath it has eroded away except for where the cairn sits?'

'Uh-huh?'

'It's sat there for many, many years while the rock has worn away beneath it.'

'Like for hundreds of years?'

'At least,' said Bob.

'Got any cool bush medicine to stop my head hurting?' she asked.

'Mrs A'll have some Panadol at the camp.' He stood up and continued walking. 'I'll get you some water.'

Jess walked behind him, clicking to Wally as she went. As they reached the trees, Bob pointed to a pitted creek bed. 'There.'

'But it's dry,' said Jess.

He squatted by the creek and pulled out a smooth, curved piece of timber from the back of his jeans. 'Coolamon,' he explained. 'Bit old-fashioned, but it works good.' Holding it like a scoop, he began to dig.

'Why do you call Opal the *debil debil* horse?' asked Jess, as she watched him. 'Do you really think she's cursed?'

'There are lots of old stories,' said Bob. 'About the yarramin with the devil in their bellies. But they were just made up to keep the little ones safe, back in the days of the massacres.'

'Maybe it's just me that's cursed,' said Jess miserably.

They both sat by the hole in silence. At the bottom, a pool of water formed slowly.

Bob reached in and scooped some out with the piece of wood. 'Drink,' he said.

While she slurped at the water, he talked. 'Lotta my people's culture been lost over the years. The songlines are all broken, and the knowledge lost. I don't know everything, but I know there's something not right with that horse of yours.'

'Do you reckon opals are bad-luck stones?'

Bob looked thoughtful. 'Opals are tied up with the creation of fire in some places, also with the butterfly. My people's way, a big pelican ancestor spilled them from his beak, along with fish for the rivers. Then another pelican was pecking at the stones and created fire.' He paused. 'Another fire story has the galah carrying a firestick and dropping embers everywhere to make opal. The opal was bad luck and not used to make tools – it had to be left in the ground.'

He scribbled a stick in the sand with a troubled look on his face. 'Why'd you reckon that creek back your way is called Slaughtering Creek, Jess?'

'Maybe there was an abattoir near it once?' The name had always made her envisage cows' blood flowing down the river. It had always made her uncomfortable somehow.

Bob gave her a look.

The realisation hit Jess like a tonne of bricks. 'Oh my God, was there a massacre?'

He shrugged.

'Everything bad happens down there! Diamond's accident. The bite from Rocko – Shara's arm. The fight we had. Opal in the floodwater . . .' Jess drew a slow breath. 'It's a bad site, isn't it?' she whispered. 'I was right, it's cursed. It really is cursed . . . bad spirits are there.'

'It's not my country, Jess. I dunno what went on there.'

Jess suddenly remembered something. She fumbled in her pocket and brought out the small floater that the willy-willy had revealed. 'Look what I found this morning,' she said, holding it out to him. 'I thought it might be some sort of sign.'

'What is it?' Bob asked, looking puzzled.

'An opal,' said Jess, surprised that he didn't recognise it. She showed him how the solid crystal centre gleamed with colour when she tilted it in the sunlight.

Bob frowned, lifted the opal up to the light and squinted at it. Then he spat on it and rubbed it. 'Where'd you find it?'

'We found it at the bore. A willy-willy blew the dirt off it and there it was, shining at me.'

Bob looked baffled. 'Which bore?

It was Jess's turn to look baffled. 'I don't know, the turkey's nest, with the big windmill,' she said pointing back behind her. 'This is opal country, isn't it?'

Bob shook his head. 'Coupla hundred kays south, maybe.'

Jess felt a strange twist in her stomach.

'Nothin' but red rocks here.' Bob bent over into the waterhole he had dug, and rinsed the stone off. 'This is grey. Ironstone. Not from round here. Must have fallen outta someone's pocket.'

'Well, it wasn't mine.'

He pointed to some small marks. 'It's been split with tools, look.'

Jess felt her skin crawl when she realised who must have owned it.

Bob passed the stone back to her. 'I've found an opal brings bad luck until you either get rid of it or put it back where it came from.'

19

'JESS!' LUKE YELLED. He galloped up behind her and Bob just as they reached the new camp. He threw himself from the saddle, grabbing Legsy's reins as his feet hit the ground. 'What happened, Jess? Legsy came back without you. I've been searching everywhere. I couldn't find you!'

He grabbed her in a bear hug and Jess threw her arms around his neck. 'I'm so sorry I lost hold of Legsy. I thought he'd taken off with the brumbies!'

Luke gave her a huge squeeze and sank his face into her shoulder. 'Oh God, Jess.' He squeezed her even tighter and breathed a huge sigh of relief into her neck, then took her by the shoulders and looked her up and down. 'I thought you were dead!'

Then he noticed Wally wandering behind her. 'You found her!' He looked further afield. 'Where's Marnie?'

'She's on a truck. The ringers have got her! Lawson's so angry at me.'

'Why? It's not your fault.'

'We had a fight, a really big one. It started about Marnie, but then it was about Wally and then about Opal . . .'

'Not again,' he groaned. Then he looked at her torn clothes and began shooting questions at her. 'Those ringers didn't hurt you, did they? What happened? Where were they?'

She shook her head. 'Legsy spooked at a goat.'

Luke abruptly stopped his questions. Then he slowly turned and gave his horse a look of absolute dissatisfaction. 'You *didn't*!'

Legsy dropped his head and took a step backwards. It made Jess laugh.

'Excuse me, please,' Luke said. He took his horse aside, held his ear and gave him a quiet talking to, within earshot of Jess. 'Mate, that's no way to impress a girl; remember what we talked about? You were s'posed to go out there and make a good impression.'

Jess smiled and went to give Legsy a pat. 'He was a perfect gentleman before that happened.'

'Well, I should hope so.' He glared at his horse again and then laughed as he led Jess to the trailer, which had barely been unpacked. Shara and Grace came running out, followed by Rosie and Mrs Arnold.

Jess was bossed into a fold-out chair, and with all

the gentleness of a post-hole digger, Mrs Arnold began excavating the bits of ironbark out of her grazed leg. Despite her indignant squeals of pain, Jess was subjected to a thorough interrogation.

What were you doing riding without a helmet? Why were you riding alone? Where was Luke? Why were you riding with him in the first place – alone? On a stallion, no water, no idea where you were going, lucky you didn't die of heatstroke, not to mention dehydration, you never go anywhere, ANYWHERE, out here without water!

Grace peered over her mother's shoulder and cheered each time Mrs Arnold plucked a particularly chunky bit of tree from Jess's leg. 'Kwor, that must have hurt heaps!'

Mrs Arnold finished with some iodine and bandages from the horses' first aid kit, leaving Jess's leg bruised, pitted and puffy. Then she took Jess by both ears, yanked her face forward and pushed her hair back. 'You've got a huge egg on your head.'

'Check out the big cut,' Grace enthused.

'It really hurts. Do you have any Pana—?'

'No!' snapped Mrs Arnold, slopping more water and iodine on the cut. 'Christ, how am I gonna explain this to your parents, Jessica Fairley?'

'Are you going to send me home?' asked Jess, lifting her head with alarm.

Mrs Arnold yanked it back down. 'Do you wanna go home?'

'Ow! No!'

'I'd rather wait a few days and send you home in one piece,' Mrs Arnold grumbled. As she let Jess lift her head again she put a hand in front of her face. 'How many fingers?'

'Six,' said Jess.

Mrs Arnold packed up her things and headed back to her trailer. 'Smart alec.'

'Thanks, Mrs A.'

'Hmph.'

Jess stayed in the fold-out chair and stared into the fire, watching embers waft into the air and float away into the late afternoon sky. The heat from it made her eyes feel scratchy. A stick fell, and sparks flew up as the frame of the fire collapsed. Dust seemed to have crept into every part of her, through her matted hair, along the creases of her skin and inside her clothes. She thought about how much energy it would take to get herself down to the creek for a wash. Too much energy . . .

So she thought instead of her conversation with Bob, trying to make sense of it.

Mrs Arnold pottered about near the trailer. 'Where's my bloody rolling pin?' she muttered.

Ryan, Jess noticed, sat a small distance away, on the

ground with his head in his hands, looking totally and utterly dejected. His hat lay upside down at his boots and she could see his hands shaking. She got up and walked towards him to tell him it wasn't his fault, that Lawson was a bastard.

'Leave him,' said Mrs Arnold from behind her.

'But—'

Mrs Arnold shook her head. 'Not now.' She pointed to a log, indicating Jess should sit. 'You need to rest.'

Reluctantly, Jess did as she was told and sat there idly watching everyone else work, trying to ignore the throb in her leg and the pounding of her head.

'Do you know how Slaughtering Creek got its name?' she asked Shara, as she took the cup of tea her friend offered her.

Shara sat on the ground next to her. 'A whole lot of Aboriginal people were killed there, years ago. Didn't you know that?'

'No, I thought it was because cows got slaughtered there,' said Jess, bewildered at how easily the answer came.

'Eight policemen were sent out there to deliberately kill them,' said Shara. 'We learned about it in History. They lured the Aborigines into the bush and then shot them.'

'Why?'

'The history books don't say,' shrugged Shara. 'But that's how the creek got its name.'

Jess sat there, aghast. 'So people like Bob, Lindy, just . . . shot.'

'Yep.'

'No wonder it's such a bad place,' said Jess. 'It's got bad spirits.' Then she mumbled, 'Opal's cursed.'

'No, she's not,' said Shara. 'There has to be a proper scientific explanation for what's happening to her.'

Jess was unconvinced. 'Well, no vet seems to be able to work it out.'

Eventually they saw the cattle wandering towards the bore in the distance and watched as they watered in small groups and then wandered off onto the reserve to graze. The riders began coming into camp, looking for dinner. Luke and Bob came back from the horse break.

Lindy made a beeline for Jess and crouched in front of her. 'You okay, matey? What happened, did those ringers chase you?'

The kindness in her voice made Jess suddenly feel exhausted and she realised she wasn't okay at all. 'They saw me. I thought they were going to come after me. I was scared. I bolted.' Before Jess knew it, she was telling Lindy about the incident with Dave the night before.

After listening intently without saying much, Lindy gave Jess a rub on the knee and stood up to head for the trailer. From inside it, Jess could hear Lindy, Bob and Mrs Arnold murmuring.

Luke, looking tired and filthy, came and sat quietly next to her, his elbows on his knees and his hat in his hands.

After a while, Bob stepped out of the trailer and sat on the ground nearby, patting one of Lindy's dogs as it nuzzled under his arm. The campsite went strangely quiet.

Lindy reappeared, disappeared again, and then walked towards the campfire with a large bundle of green leafy branches in her arms. She dropped them by Jess's feet and went back to the trailer. Jess watched curiously as she fetched an old copper washbowl, brought it to the fire and began scooping coals into it.

Lindy carried the bowl over to Jess and sat in front of her. She began tearing small clumps of mulga leaves off the branches and placing them over the coals, poking at them with a stick until smoke billowed up, thick and silvery. Then she began a quiet, gentle chant, pushing the dish towards Jess and motioning for her to lean over it.

'Are you smoking me?' asked Jess.

Lindy smiled, and Jess let the grey plumes float into her skin as Lindy fanned them with a branch. The smoke seeped into her clothes and swam through her hair, covering her with its softness. She closed her eyes and breathed deeply, inhaling the intricate scent, feeling the vibrations of Lindy's song and letting it heal her.

The stress and anxiety Jess held for Opal floated away with the smoke, and her bruises stopped aching. She opened her mouth and exhaled the anger she held for Lawson. A warm smoky blanket wrapped around the sadness in her heart that Diamond had left there, softening and soothing.

She sat like that for several minutes, with her eyes closed, and it felt good.

Jess opened her eyes after a little while and watched the twisting plumes of smoke carry her demons away. She felt spellbound, a bit light-headed.

Lindy kept singing and then pushed the dish towards Luke. She motioned him forward and he did as he was told, closing his eyes and inhaling cautiously, his elbows on his knees and his chin in his hands.

Lindy took more leaves and placed them over the coals. She snapped off a small branch and waved the smoke all around him. After a while she stood and kept fanning the smoke as she walked behind him to pull his shirt up and over his head.

As Luke's shirt peeled from his body, Jess noticed that he still wore the moonstone pendant she'd given him ages ago.

Lindy waved the smoke at his ribs and Luke put a

hand over them and scowled. Lindy continued to fan the smoke over his body, and he reluctantly lifted his arms and let her have her way, looking sideways at Jess and winking.

Grace walked into the camp with a saddle in her arms and a bridle over her shoulder. 'What are you doing?' she asked loudly.

Bob put his finger to his lips, then answered her quietly. 'Smoking – she's cleaning us from bad energy. Like washing your spirit, if you've been near a ghost or a place that's no good.'

One by one, Lindy went around to the rest of the group, Ryan, Grace, Shara and then Rosie, performing the same ceremony.

When Lindy finished, Rosie began to softly sing the pony song. Lindy looked at her, with her perfectly groomed nails and fresh lip gloss in the middle of the outback. 'Crikey, Rosie, is that the only song you know?'

Although Jess had vowed she never wanted to hear the pony song again as long as she lived, she had the sudden urge to join her.

Shara grabbed a chunky stick and began to bang on a metal bowl.

Bob stood up to dance in the smoke, chanting in his own language, which went surprisingly well with Kasey's lyrics. He stamped his feet like a cranky emu and held out a hand to Grace, who jumped up and joined him. 'This is fun!' she said.

'You've all gone troppo,' said Mrs Arnold, walking past with a huge pot in her arms. 'You sound bloody terrible.'

Jess sang even louder.

Luke rolled over the log and grabbed her in a rugby tackle, laughing and rumbling her to the ground. He growled wordlessly in her ear, sending goosebumps up her arms. She giggled and rolled with him until they both lay on their backs, staring up at the late afternoon sky.

When Rosie started singing the third round of the pony song, Jess stopped singing and lay there, acutely aware of Luke beside her. He lay with his hands behind his head, chest rising in a slow rhythm as he breathed. The moonstone sat in the hollow just beneath his Adam's apple.

'What day is it?' asked Jess.

'Tuesday,' said Luke. 'Or Friday? Something like that.'

Jess sighed. 'I think I missed my birthday.'

'When was your birthday?'

'Wednesday. Or Monday, or something like that.'

Luke laughed.

Jess heard the hollow twang of a banjo being plucked. The fingerpicking was intermittent and erratic, as if the instrument was being tuned.

'How old are you now?' asked Luke.

'Ummm . . .' Jess mumbled. 'Sixteen.'

The banjo suddenly burst into a continuous lively roll.

'Hey, that's Harry's banjo!' Jess sat up.

Ryan sat looking into the fire with a banjo on his lap, one foot resting on a bucket. His right hand was a blur of plucking fingers and his left moved easily up and down the fretboard while the rest of him was motionless.

He saw Jess's head pop up from behind the log and began to pluck the tune for 'Happy Birthday'. Somehow he managed to make it sound sad.

By the time Rosie, Grace and Shara got to 'Happy birthday, dear Je-ssi-caaa,' Luke was staring at Jess with an unquestionably wicked grin. 'Sweet sixteen, ay?' he said, so quietly she barely heard him.

She looked at his grubby face and shaggy, dusty hair. 'And never been kissed; it's ridiculous.'

'Let's go for a swim in the river,' he whispered.

20

LUKE LED JESS to a small clearing. He ripped off his shirt and boots and waded into the river in his jeans. When it reached his waist, he sank down, disappearing into the murky water, leaving ripples and bubbles on the surface.

Jess opted for jeans and singlet and waded in after him. She squealed as two arms wrapped around her legs and tried to pull her under. She let herself fall and felt the cool water rush over her upper body, neck and then face.

When they surfaced together, Jess's fingers twined through Luke's. They stood facing each other, chest-deep in the water, grinning stupidly at each other.

'You still wear that moonstone.'

He nodded.

'Does it give you good dreams?'

His grin broadened. 'You have no idea.'

Jess felt herself blush. 'Mrs Arnold's going to follow us down here, you know.'

Luke stopped smiling and looked at her with a face she couldn't read.

She slid her arms around his neck, stood on tiptoe and kissed him quickly on the lips. He pulled her close and kissed her back. Then they stood there with their foreheads together, nose to nose, grinning.

'I've been wanting to do that for so long,' whispered Luke.

She kissed him again. 'How long?'

'Ever since you threw yourself all over me in the ute at Harry's place.'

A sudden memory flashed in Jess's mind – jumping into the back of Harry's ute, and accidentally falling into Luke's lap; she'd nearly died of embarrassment. She pulled away and scoffed. 'I did not. You are so on yourself.'

'You did. You wanted me *bad*,' he laughed, pulling her back into his arms.

She pushed at his chest. 'You wanted *me* bad.'

He rolled his eyes. 'All right, I did,' he confessed.

Jess put her arms back around his neck. 'So am I your first-ever kiss?'

'No.'

'Really? Who else? You said you wanted to kiss me for years!'

He gave her a teasing smile.

'Who? Tell me!'

'Jealous?'

'*Tell me.*'

'It was a long time ago.'

'How long?'

''Bout fourteen years.'

'No one's kissed you for fourteen years?'

'Sounds a bit tragic when you say it like that.'

'No wonder you like hammering people.'

Luke's mood changed instantly. 'I don't *like* hammering people.' He reached around his neck and peeled away her arms, taking her by the hands again and giving her a hurt look.

'Yeah, I know, but you . . . just seem so comfortable with violence.'

'Seen a lot of it, I s'pose.' He let go of her, waded out of the water and began towelling himself with his shirt.

Jess followed him onto the riverbank. 'Are you angry?'

Luke sat heavily on the sand and put his elbows on his knees without answering.

She knelt down in front of him. 'All that fighting really freaks me out.'

'I was looking after you when I hit Dave.' Luke ran the back of his hand over her cheek, a dark look in his eyes. 'It doesn't stop, you know. When they get drunk like that, they just go on and on until they've destroyed everything around them. I'll *never* be like that. I was in total control. I knew when to stop.'

Jess looked at him, at his gorgeous seventeen-year-old face, boyish and playful, framed by a wild mop of messy hair. 'I know you're not like that.'

'I'm not,' he promised.

'I know.'

Luke breathed a sigh and looked relieved. 'I don't need to get into fights, because I've got my life together now. I don't do that stuff anymore. Not unless someone deserves it—'

'Luke, will you shut up?'

He shut up and looked at her, frowning.

She shoved him.

He shoved her back, smiling.

Jess grabbed his hands and he rolled onto his back, pulling her down with him. Then he was kissing her again, and she was kissing him back with her whole heart.

Until Mrs Arnold came crashing through the trees. '*Ahem*!'

21

DARKNESS WAS FALLING as Jess stood towelling her hair in the back of the truck. Outside, she heard the banjo and easy banter stop suddenly. Rosie, Shara and Grace pushed their way hurriedly into the trailer and all but the cows went strangely quiet. Lawson and Stanley were riding into the camp.

The four girls jostled for a view out of the small window as Lawson dismounted and tied Chocky to a sturdy tree. Without so much as loosening the colt's girth, he marched directly to Ryan and kicked a bootful of dirt at him. 'Get up!' he yelled. 'Get up and tell me where those ringers have taken my good mare!'

Ryan – wisely – stayed seated. He held up his hands defensively. 'I don't know. I told you, I have no idea.'

Lindy put a hand on Lawson's arm. 'You can't blame him, Lawson. Ryan can't control what the other men did.'

Lawson stood there, breathing heavily, and then

walked away. He sat on the other side of the fire and tore off his hat. 'What's for dinner?' he snarled.

'It's not cooked yet,' said Mrs Arnold. 'We're running late, just like you.'

'Maybe you'll think twice before you go putting alcohol in it this time,' said Lawson.

'What the—'

'This run was supposed to be alcohol-free.'

'It was for cooking!'

'Well, they still found it, Jude.'

Mrs Arnold's mouth was a thin line as she grabbed for a pile of tea towels. Wrapping them around her hands, she heaved her enormous pot of half-cooked stew from the fire and marched to the trailer. 'You can all go bloody hungry tonight,' she said, and kicked the door shut behind her.

'Great,' said Lindy. 'Now you've upset the cook.'

Lawson crammed his hat back on and stalked off.

With Lawson gone, the girls stepped cautiously one by one out of the trailer and continued with their jobs.

Jess shook her head with disbelief. 'Lawson is such a pig. My father would never talk to my mother like—'

'He's upset about his horse,' said Stanley. 'Give the man a break.'

Jess looked at Luke, who sat tight-faced against the wheel of the trailer, tapping one foot anxiously against the other. She went over and sat by him. 'You okay?'

'I need to get away from all this,' he said stiffly. 'I'm gonna go crash in the back of the ute.' He walked off into the darkness.

Jess went back to the fire and stood next to Rosie while she added more logs. 'Well, that went well.'

Rosie burst out laughing, then quickly dissolved into sobs.

'Heyyy,' said Shara, putting an arm around her.

'He *is* such a pig,' said Grace. 'How dare he talk to Mum like that? I can't believe Dad stuck up for him. I'm never getting married.'

Lindy sat opposite them, her serious face illuminated by the flames. She picked up a stick and poked at the fire.

'How come Lawson always listens to you?' Grace asked her.

She looked up. 'Because he's a kind and decent man.'

'How can you say that?' asked Jess.

'How can you not?' said Lindy. 'I thought you of all people would understand how he's feeling right now, Jess. That man has spent all day droving my cattle instead of chasing after his mare because it's the decent and honourable thing to do. If you want him to show you some respect, then all four of you need to get off your butts and earn it.'

Jess, Grace, Rosie and Shara all sat there, dumbfounded.

'Why didn't he just ask *us* to drove the cattle?' said Grace eventually. 'Oh yeah, that's right – because we're all girls. We're only good for cooking and cleaning.'

'Shut up, Grace,' said Rosie.

'I'm going to bed,' groaned Jess.

Jess lay in the peak of the trailer with her leg still aching and her stomach screaming for some food. It was so quiet outside that she could hear the crackle of the fire. Mrs Arnold lay in her cot, motionless except for her fingers, which drummed angrily on her arm. The incessant tapping noise was beginning to drive Jess nuts, and she lay there fantasising about daring to throw a pillow at her.

There was a bang on the trailer door. 'I want everyone to come outside for a talk,' said Lindy's voice.

'This oughta be good,' grumbled Mrs Arnold.

Jess dragged herself out of bed.

One by one, Lindy brought everyone from their hiding places. Lawson stood with his arms folded, looking surly, and refused to sit down. Mrs Arnold wouldn't leave the doorway of the trailer. 'I can hear everything from here,' she said obstinately.

Jess rejoined Shara, Rosie and Grace, who sat along

a log with blankets wrapped around them. Bob stood quietly in the shadows, Luke took one of the fold-out chairs, Stan and Ryan stood alongside each other, both with arms folded across their chests.

Lindy held up a short thick stick. 'No one talks unless they hold the stick,' she instructed, then she began a lecture. 'What is wrong with you mob? You guys are all kin, mostly. You should be pulling together. Someone's done wrong by your family member and you're not banding together. I don't get it.' She held the stick out. 'Who wants it?'

Everyone stared at it in silence.

She gave it a coaxing wave. 'User-friendly.'

No one took the stick.

Lindy spoke again. 'If anyone's to blame for those ringers, it's me – I hired them. They were my staff, my responsibility. I just wish I'd got rid of them quicker.'

Ryan stepped forward and took the stick. 'I didn't know those blokes well enough. I thought they were okay. I wouldn't have asked you to put them on otherwise.'

Mrs Arnold marched out and grabbed the stick from Ryan. 'Not my fault one of 'em raided my stash.' She stomped over to Lawson and shoved the stick at him. He refused to unfold his arms, and she poked him with it.

'Hey!' he said, angrily.

Lindy coughed. 'Um, that's not really how it's used.'

Mrs Arnold thrust it insistently at Lawson again, and this time he snatched it from her. 'What do you want me to say?'

Mrs Arnold snatched it back. 'You can start by apologising,' she snapped.

'To who?'

'Don't you speak while I got the stick.'

'You snatched it off me!'

She thrust it back at him.

'I don't want it now.'

'You guys are like children,' said Rosie.

'You're a disgrace!' Grace jumped up, marched over and held out her hand for the stick. Lawson ripped it from Mrs Arnold's hand and gave it to her.

'We're not just useless girls, you know,' said Grace. 'You could've asked us to help with the cattle. Me and Jess and Sharsy and . . . I s'pose even Rosie. We could help Lindy drove the cattle while the men go and look for Marnie. You could take the ute.'

'Marnie'll be at the saleyards by now,' said Stanley.

'Oi!' Grace waved the stick at her father to shut him up, then handed it back to Lawson and waited for his response.

'Marnie's microchipped and branded. I've reported her stolen to the authorities, so she should get picked up if she goes through any saleyards. But the ringers would know that.' He shook his head. 'I just hope they don't shoot her. She's too nice a horse.'

The camp fell silent. After a while, Jess stepped forward and took the stick from Lawson's dejected grasp. 'Let us help with the cattle, Lawson. We can do it. You should be off looking for Marnie.'

He held his hands in the air. 'Looking where?'

'I don't know, maybe go back to where I saw their truck and follow the tracks?'

Lawson gave Lindy a *what-do-you-think* look.

She nodded. 'I think it's a good idea. You got some good riders here. They'll be all right if they listen up.'

Lawson looked unconvinced. 'Fifteen hundred head of cattle to move?'

'They're very quiet, old cows mostly. I'm sure the girls can handle them.'

Jess could see Lawson turning things over in his head. Finally he gave a sigh of resignation. 'You're the boss. If you don't mind me taking off. If you're happy to ride with a bunch of kids—'

'We'll be right,' said Lindy. 'Won't we, girls?'

Grace jumped up and punched the air. 'Yeah, baby!'

'We're going droving,' cried Shara, jumping up and grabbing Jess, Rosie and Grace. The four girls jumped around in a circle.

'No more stockies' jocks!' Rosie rejoiced.

'Hang on a minute,' said Mrs Arnold. 'You can't all go. I still need help to pack up camp. I'm going into town for supplies tomorrow.' She looked at the four girls, who were still hand in hand, jumping for joy. 'Someone's gotta stay with me.'

The girls all stopped and stared at each other.

'I'll stay,' Jess volunteered eventually. 'I wouldn't mind going into town and finding a phone.'

'Good,' said Mrs Arnold.

'Right, that's settled then,' said Lindy. 'Grace, Rosie and Shara can ride with me. You blokes can hunt down those ringers and get Marnie back.'

Bob sidled up to Lawson. 'Want me to come? Might find some tracks.'

'That'd be great, Bob,' said Lawson, slapping him on the shoulder and suddenly sounding more positive. 'We'll take the ute, put the motorbike on the back.'

'I'll come too,' said Ryan, and the hopeful chatter that filled the camp instantly fell away to uneasy silence.

Lawson took a while to answer; when he did, his tone was cold and unwelcoming. 'I think you've already done enough.'

'I want to help get the mare back. I want to find Dave and Clarkey.' Ryan looked at Lawson earnestly. 'I want to make things right.'

The camp remained silent as a thick slick of tension

ran between the two men. The fire snapped and popped and the generator hummed, but no one spoke.

'You've got an awful lot of stuff to make right, Ryan,' Lawson said eventually.

'So let me help you. I know some of the places they go, some of the people they associate with.'

Lawson was still cold and quiet.

'I didn't mean for this to happen, Lawson. I came out here to reconcile with you. I thought these guys were okay. I was wrong.'

When Lawson replied, he was surprisingly controlled. 'You got to be more careful about who you spend your time with.'

Ryan looked straight at him. 'Then let me spend time with you.'

22

JESS SCRUBBED THE LAST of the morning breakfast dishes after eating half a pig, nearly an entire loaf of bread and a mountain of scrambled eggs. Upsetting the cook on a droving run, she had discovered, was a foolhardy thing to do on Lawson's part. Mrs Arnold had locked the entire food supply in a large metal box, stored it under her cot and slept on it all night, refusing to yield to the hungry demands of her fellow campers. By morning Lawson had lost all popularity and the entire camp milled around anxiously waiting for breakfast.

As she watched Shara, Rosie and Grace ride out, Jess wondered how long it would take to get scurvy without a morsel of fresh food. She could hear the cattle crooning loudly as they bustled around, waiting to get out and graze for the day.

'You got the rough end of the pineapple today, Jess,'

said Mrs Arnold, bundling up her cooking gear and packing it into the trailer.

'At least a pineapple would have a bit of vitamin C,' Jess murmured.

'What?'

'Nothing. I don't mind,' said Jess. 'I really want to ring the station and see how Opal is. I was going to ask Lawson if I could borrow his phone, but he wasn't really in the mood last night.'

'Oh, I meant to tell you,' said Mrs Arnold from inside the trailer. 'He rang the station about her.'

Jess rushed to the doorway. 'What did they say?'

'Lawson was pretty vague. He just said she was the same, or something like that. Like you say, he wasn't really in the mood for talking. Nor was I for that matter. Sorry I can't tell you any more than that, love.'

Jess's heart lifted a little. At least Opal was still alive. Maybe she was even getting a bit better. She imagined the filly, gleaming in the sunlight, trotting about with the other brumby foals. She set about packing with renewed energy, keen to find a phone as soon as possible and hear every detail of Opal's health, firsthand.

Lawson helped Luke and Ryan load a motorbike onto the back of the ute and tie it down with ropes. Then he jumped in the driver's seat. Bob disappeared into the passenger side of the ute, while Luke and Ryan jumped on the back and stood holding the roll bar.

'I hope they find Marnie,' said Jess, as she watched them take off down the road, leaving a trail of dust behind them.

'Don't fancy their chances,' said Mrs Arnold.

Without the other girls, it took a good hour to pack up after everyone. Mrs Arnold made Jess sort out the unholy mess the girls had made in the back of the gooseneck, and to Jess's dismay, this produced a whole new load of dirty washing.

'We can find a laundromat in town while no one else is looking,' said Mrs Arnold, winking at her.

Jess shook sand and horse hair out of Grace's sleeping bag and rolled it and the others up. She swept out the peak of the trailer and shoved any clean clothes she could find into duffle bags. She bagged up rubbish, rearranged saddles and folded up chairs and camping tables. With the men having taken the ute, they needed to find even more space to pack the swags, horse rugs and all manner of other gear. Finally, when they could barely squeeze in another item, Jess and Mrs Arnold lifted the tailgate of the trailer and latched it closed.

An hour's bumpy drive over the dirt track and another hour up the highway, Mrs Arnold pulled into a large highway truckstop. It had the usual franchised burger joints, souvenir shops and food halls catering for busloads of tourists. Mrs Arnold found a spot towards the back of the huge car park and pulled on the brake. 'Should be able to get supplies here,' she said.

Jess sat in the passenger seat, hunched over her mobile. She waited impatiently as it struggled and failed to find a network. 'Useless thing,' she said, tossing it back into her bag. She hopped out and stretched. 'I'm going to look for a landline.'

'Try the servo. I'm going to the mini-mart.'

Jess wandered into the cool, air-conditioned servo. It was enormous, set up with several individual shopfronts offering everything a bored and weary traveller could wish for. A newsagent presented racks of books and newspapers before shelves of trinkets, stationery and souvenirs. There were about four different food bars with glass-fronted bain-maries, some with greasy processed food, others with gourmet burgers wrapped in paper and stacked in neat rows.

Jess scanned the various food menus for anything vaguely tempting, wrinkled her nose and decided to get something fresh from the mini-mart. She searched across what seemed like acres of tables and chairs for a public phone, but before she located one, another shopfront caught her eye.

GENUINE QLD OPALS
FINE OPAL JEWELLERY
AND LOOSE STONES

Jess wandered over and peered at the glistening gems through the polished glass. They were all so different. There was a small cluster of whitish stones, shaped and polished to look almost like a clutch of tiny eggs. Another opal was cut to a diamond shape with mostly blues and yellows. She moved her head from side to side and watched the different play of colours in the changing angle of light. Then she noticed another, which was black with streaks of fiery red.

'Beautiful, aren't they?' A well-groomed man in a shirt and tie smiled charmingly at her, his hands behind his back.

'I love opals,' said Jess.

'Come in and have a look.'

Jess knew he was spruiking and she inwardly berated herself for playing straight into his sales pitch. 'I actually have to make a phone call,' she said, wanting to escape.

'You can use our phone, if you like,' he said. 'Come on in.'

'Okay, just quickly,' she said, following him into the shop.

The man walked behind a counter. 'We have lots of different styles,' he said. 'Black opals . . . white opals . . . boulder opals . . .' He began pulling out velvet-covered trays of necklaces and bracelets.

Jess was about to ask him about the promised phone call, when another cabinet caught her attention. 'I find those ones more interesting,' she said, pointing at a shelf of loose and roughly cut stones on flat sheets of old cardboard in a purposely rustic display.

The man whipped the other trays away and began pulling out individual stones. He picked through various clumps, streaked with blues, whites and greens. 'The play on this one is quite beautiful,' he said, turning it around in the light.

It was beautiful, but a different piece of rock caught Jess's attention: a jagged grey layer of stone around a solid opal centre, not unlike the one she had found near the trough. 'What about that one?' she said, pointing at it through the glass.

'Ah yes, the Yowah nuts,' said the man, pulling the entire tray out. 'A man brought those in only yesterday. Getting harder to find these days.'

There were only a few pieces, five in total, but the one Jess had already seen nearly made her heart stop. She patted her top jacket pocket. 'Where is it?' she mumbled to herself. Then she found what she was searching for in the front of her jeans. She pulled it out and opened her fist, revealing an almost identical piece of stone.

She took the piece from the tray and pressed its cut surface against that of the opal she had found by the trough. The halves fused together so perfectly that barely a crack showed where the stone had been split. Jess stared at the man with an open mouth. 'How weird is that?'

The man's forehead wrinkled into deep furrows. 'Snap,' he said. 'How bizarre!'

'Where did your piece come from?'

'Yowah – it's the only place in the world where opals form like that,' said the salesman. 'Where'd you find yours?'

'Next to a water trough, out on the stock route,' said Jess slowly. 'Hey, that guy didn't leave his name or number, did he?'

'Somewhere . . .' The man looked thoughtful and then fumbled around for a bit. He found a receipt book under a pile of papers and began leafing through it.

Jess saw the name *David* on the receipt before the salesman did. Dave's surname was Rawlins. She could feel herself beginning to hyperventilate. 'Can I have his details,' she squeaked, 'please?'

A look of uncertainty crossed the man's face.

Jess put her hand firmly on his book, holding it open on Dave's receipt. 'Either that or I'll have to ring the police,' she said, hoping all the tales she'd heard about opals and money-laundering were true. 'I think the man is a horse thief.'

The tales must have been true. 'There shouldn't be any need for the police,' the man said quickly, and scrawled the details on a piece of paper. He pushed it towards her, looking tense.

'Can I buy this one?' Jess pulled out her wallet, still with the cash for Opal inside, and prayed it wouldn't be too expensive. She reeled at the irony. 'I've been saving up to buy an Opal.'

'Maybe you should just take it and get going,' said the man, handing it to her and closing his receipt book. He began bundling the trays and loose stones back into the display cabinet.

Jess bolted out the door with the opals in one hand and the address in the other, nearly flying into the path of an oncoming Winnebago. She skidded to a halt and darted across the car park to the front doors of the mini-mart.

'*MRS ARNOLD!*' she screamed at the top of her lungs.

'What?' said Mrs Arnold from one of the checkouts. She continued to load groceries onto the conveyor belt. 'No need to yell, I'm right here.'

'Mrs Arnold!' Jess panted. 'I found him. I found the ringers!' She waved the paper at her and hopped from one foot to another.

Back in the servo, Jess paced anxiously back and forth while Mrs Arnold tried to reach Lawson on his satellite phone. 'Stan!' she finally shouted into the phone.

Mrs Arnold squinted at the paper and read the address repeatedly, eventually spelling each word letter by letter, then using phonetic code when her husband still couldn't hear her.

'Yowah!' she yelled into the phone. 'Yankee, Oscar, Whisky, Alpha . . . No, Yankee, as in Y, as in *WHY don't you ever wear your hearing aid?*'

She finally emerged from the phone booth looking exhausted. 'Useless satellite,' she said in an annoyed tone. 'Didn't help that he's as deaf as a post.'

'What did he say?' asked Jess. 'Was Lawson there? What did Lawson say?'

'He's off on the motorbike. Stan's going to go and find him.' She shook her head. 'Course, he didn't have a pen. He's used his finger to write the address on the bonnet of the ute, in the dust. Hopefully it'll still be there after driving around for the next few hours, in even more dust, trying to find Lawson.'

'Wish we had another sat phone – we could text it to him.'

'You can do it on the internet. There's a website you can use,' said Mrs Arnold.

'Where there are tourists, there are usually internet cafes!' said Jess.

There were two computers at the far end of the dining area in the servo. Jess bought an hour's internet time and booted up the computer. Out of pure habit, she logged into her Yahoo account, then tried googling for satellite phone companies.

'What type of phone does he have?' Jess asked Mrs Arnold. 'There are different brands.'

Mrs Arnold pulled a *stuffed-if-I-know* face.

Jess scanned through phone blogs, Facebook pages and FAQ pages on satellite phones. 'It could be anything,' she groaned. 'I'm so dumb at this. We need tech support!'

Just then a small orange pop-up appeared at the bottom of her Yahoo home screen. *Elliot is online.*

'Elliot!' cried Jess, clicking on the pop-up and bringing up the messenger.

HI ELLIOT! IT'S JESS.

hi jessica. how are the cows?

CATTLE ARE GREAT. DO U KNOW HOW TO SEND

TEXT MESSAGES TO A SATELLITE PHONE?

is it iridium pvd?

Jess and Mrs Arnold exchanged more *stuffed-if-I-know* glances.

WOTZ THAT?

Personal voice and data delivery – 66 leo satellites – very cool.

CAN U HELP US GET A MESSAGE TO LAWSON'S PHONE?

Sure. He's on my fixed rst.

DOES THAT MEAN YOU HAVE HIS NUMBER?

Affirmative

'He is such a geek!' Jess took the receipt from Mrs Arnold and began typing Dave's address.

Is grace there with you?

NO, SHE'S RIDING

can u say hello to her from elliot?

Jess and Mrs Arnold exchanged further *stuffed-if-I-know* glances, followed by *surely-not* looks and *how-sweet* gestures.

'Maybe Grace is on his fixed RST too,' Jess chuckled.

'Better not be,' Mrs Arnold growled.

CAN U TEXT THAT NAME AND ADDRESS TO LAWSON'S SAT PHONE?

i already have

THANKS ELLIOT, UR THE BEST.

The afternoon was the longest of Jess's life. Even the thrill of making a nutritious, vitamin-C-packed lunch with crunchy raw vegetables from the mini-mart didn't help it go any faster. After feeding the riders and helping them to swap horses, she drove with Mrs Arnold to the night camp and spent hours scrubbing green slime out of the water troughs and refilling them for the cattle at the designated bore. She rolled out miles of electric tape with Bob and helped count the cattle. Shara, Grace and Rosie came in to where they were settling for the night, leading their horses, looking totally exhilarated.

'You should see Lindy's dogs work,' Grace enthused. 'One just jumped up and bit this cow on the neck when it wouldn't move; it was awesome! I'm gonna get Dad to buy me a smithy when we get home.'

'I broke my gel tips,' Rosie moaned, leading Slinger past and studying her fingernails. 'I knew I should've got acrylic.'

Grace screwed up her face. 'Who's going to see your fingernails out here?'

'I am,' Rosie retorted. 'Just because you have no concept of self-presentation, or personal hygiene.'

Grace blew a raspberry at her and walked away, whistling to Lindy's dogs.

As Jess helped them with their horses, she told them about the opal she had found. Soon they were all sitting around the campfire, waiting, waiting, for the men to arrive. As eight o' clock gave away to nine, both Mrs Arnold and Jess started getting nervous. They speculated about all sorts of possible confrontations that may have taken place.

'Maybe we shouldn't have given the address to Lawson,' said Jess. 'He was too angry. We should have rung the police.'

'Lawson can handle himself,' said Mrs Arnold, not sounding entirely convinced of that.

'Luke shouldn't have gone. He already had a blow-up with Dave,' Jess fretted. 'He'll get in another fight.' Then she thought of Lawson and Ryan. 'This is just really bad. They're all going to kill each other. Maybe we should drive back into town and try to get hold of Elliot again, see if he's heard from Lawson.'

Mrs Arnold shook her head. Then Jess saw her eyebrows lower into a curious frown as though she was remembering something. 'Elliot said to say hello to you, Grace,' she said, in a tone that suggested her daughter explain.

'Did he?' said Grace, looking suddenly busy and distracted. 'Why?'

Her mother maintained her stare. Grace picked up her saddle and bridle and walked to the back of the trailer. 'Do you know if we have any anti-gall girths? That horse was a bit ticklish this morning.'

Mrs Arnold glanced suspiciously at Jess, who answered with another *don't-ask-me* shrug.

Just as Jess thought she couldn't hold her eyes open any longer, they heard the ute rumbling along the dirt track, and the unmistakeable sound of a float's towball bouncing on the coupling, a horse's hooves clanging about in the back. Headlights waved across the open grassy plains.

Everyone jumped up.

'They're back!' cried Jess. 'They've got a float – they've got Marnie!'

The ute stopped and Jess raced to the front door of the float and wrenched it open. She shone a torch inside and a set of soft, long-lashed eyes peered at her. 'Marnie!' Jess shone the torch all over her, looking for any signs of damage. The mare was sweaty but otherwise looked fine.

The girls crowded around as Lawson emerged from the driver's side with a wide grin on his face. 'Where's Jessica?' he demanded.

Jess was shoved to the front of the crowd and before she knew it, Lawson was swinging her around in a big happy bear-hug, so that she could hardly breathe.

'Told you opals were good-luck stones,' she laughed.

'You're a good girl, Jessica,' he said, hoisting her high into the air. 'I don't know how I'm gonna repay you.'

'Just give me my filly back,' Jess said, smiling down at him.

Lawson dropped her like a bag of rocks.

23

BY THE NEXT MORNING, all of Lawson's gratitude to Jess seemed to have vanished.

Ryan, on the other hand, seemed to have totally redeemed himself. Marnie had been found on a remote Yowah property, the discovery of which now seemed to be taken for granted. Jess had spent the evening listening to tales of how Ryan had heroically wrestled Dave to the ground, while Luke and Lawson rang the cops, caught Marnie and loaded her onto a horse float to get her out of there. Both Dave and Clarkey had been charged with live-stock theft and Ryan had come home with a big black eye, which the men all seemed to view as a badge of honour.

'Looks as if we're all back to *girl* status,' said Jess, as she helped Shara fill water buckets for the horses. 'The boys get first choice of all the horses today. Lawson hasn't even included me as a rider.'

'He's just being a control freak,' said Shara. 'He can't hand over the reins to anyone.'

'Except Lindy,' said Jess, looking over at Lawson and Lindy, who stood chummily flipping through a clipboard full of paperwork together.

'What *is* her secret?' Shara wondered out loud.

'They're *together*,' said Jess. 'I saw them smooching.'

Shara pulled a face. 'Lawson? Gross me out.'

'Hey, that's it,' said Jess, almost to herself, as a realisation dawned on her. 'The way to get through to Lawson . . . *is via Lindy!*' She smiled a self-appreciating smile, picked up the two full buckets and headed for the horses. 'I'm a genius!'

'That doesn't leave a horse for Jess. Without Dave and Clarkey we need her too,' Jess heard Lindy say as she carried the buckets, sloshing with water, through the campsite.

'Just swap her over with one of the other kids after lunch,' said Lawson.

'Bit much for one horse, to ride two shifts,' said Lindy.

Jess's brain quickly clicked into gear. She knew exactly which horse she could ride, and she knew exactly how to make it happen. She hurriedly took the buckets to the horses and then raced back to the camp.

'I'll ride Wal, Lindy.'

Lawson looked up.

'Umm, if that's okay with Lawson,' she added quickly. Best let him think he had as much control over the decision as possible.

'What, with no saddle or bridle, just a piece of string around her neck?' said Lawson. 'That won't be much chop if any cattle break out.'

'I can put a saddle on her if you like,' said Jess, addressing Lawson and then switching her focus to Lindy. 'Might take a little bit to get her used to it, but not too long — twenty minutes max,' she said, brimming over with confidence. She had been tightening ropes around Wally's belly for months. The filly wasn't going to care about a girth. And she wouldn't care about Jess sitting on her — that had been going on for months too. Jess could steer without a bridle. And stop as well. She couldn't see a problem.

Lawson interrupted. 'You're very clever getting Walkabout . . . *started*, Jessica,' he said. 'But putting her on cattle is another thing altogether. If you need to gallop—'

Jess turned to Lindy again. 'None of these cows are going to run, are they? They're old-age pensioners.'

'Not all of them,' said Lindy cautiously.

'Excuse me, this is *my* horse,' said Lawson, sounding irritated, and bringing the conversation back his own way.

Jess stared at him defiantly. 'Gonna break another one of your promises?'

Lawson ignored the comment and glared back at her. 'You don't have a helmet.'

Luke walked up behind him and threw a black helmet to Jess in a classic netball toss. Lawson shot daggers at Luke, who gave him a charming smile in return.

Jess raised her eyebrows at Lawson. 'What did you bring Wally out here for?'

Lawson didn't answer her, but she could see the look of impenetrable will beginning to form on his face. She knew she had to do some fast talking. 'I'll ride her next to an experienced, older horse,' she said quickly. When his face only seemed to set harder, Jess lowered herself to begging. 'Oh, come on, Lawson. You know this is a great way to *break in* horses.'

'Well, that rules out Legsy,' he said, giving Luke a smug look.

'I'm riding the skewbald this morning,' said Luke. He smiled at Lawson. 'Oldest horse here. Guess she'll have to ride with me.'

'Better hurry up and make a decision,' said Lindy, looking amused. 'Sun's up. We gotta get these cattle out before they get restless.' Then she gave Lawson a soft-eyed look and said very quietly, 'Don't be so mean.'

Bingo!

Jess watched in amazement as Lawson's jaw slackened and his will crumbled. 'I'm not mean,' he said, sounding like a hurt schoolboy.

Lindy put one hand on Lawson's chest and cocked her head slightly to one side. 'Yes, you are, honey.'

Jess had to look away. If she caught anyone else's eye right now, she knew she would explode with laughter – and that would be political suicide with Lawson. She willed herself to keep a straight face. 'I'll accept whatever you say,' she said with as much humility as she could muster. 'You have more experience with young horses. I know you want what's best for Wally.'

'You're damn right I do,' grumbled Lawson, then gave a sigh of resignation. 'If you can have her saddled and ready to go in twenty minutes, you can ride her.'

'Thanks, Lawson!'

And Lindy!

Jess raced back to the trailer, fighting the urge to victory howl all the way. She ripped her shorts off as soon as she got inside, dived into a pair of jeans – probably Grace's, judging by the smell – and jammed on riding boots, not bothering with socks.

By the time she got outside, Luke already had a saddle and was rummaging through some gear in the back of the ute. 'What bridle do you want?'

'Just a halter,' said Jess. 'She doesn't even need that, really.'

'I reckon you should put one on her,' he said. 'Piece of string's not much use when you're galloping after cattle.'

Bob was in the horse break saddling and haltering horses. He looked curiously at Jess and Luke approaching with another saddle. 'Did I miss one?'

'I'm going to ride Wally,' said Jess, skipping past.

Bob looked surprised. 'What the boss-man think of that?'

'He's grateful for my brilliant horse-handling skills,' said Jess, smiling graciously.

Bob gave her an *as-if* look and turned back to his work.

Jess stopped and took a deep breath. It would do no good to go rushing at Wally at a thousand miles an hour. She concentrated on containing her excitement a little, then slowly approached the little Appaloosa filly. 'Come here, Wal,' she said softly, lifting the filly's head from her feed. 'You can finish that later.'

Luke walked over, ran his hand down Wally's front leg and picked up her hoof. He ran a hand around the outside rim, picked out a couple of stones, then dropped the foot. 'I'll give her a trim at lunchtime. She'll be right for this morning, though.'

'Will you teach me to do that one day?' asked Jess.

'Sure,' he said. 'Let's get her saddled for now. What do you want me to do?'

'Maybe grab the skewbald and bring him over,' said Jess. She began leading Wally away from the other horses. Once there was a good distance, she took the saddle from Luke's arms.

She turned to Wally and showed her the saddlecloth. The filly sniffed it a few times, interested in the smell of sweat from several other horses, then lifted her tail, farted, and tried to reach down and snatch at a piece of grass.

'She doesn't seem too worried,' said Luke.

Jess ran the cloth over Wally's wither, up her neck, down over her shoulder and then along her back. She dropped the lead rope and let it fall at Wally's feet as she moved further along.

Once she had rubbed the cloth over both sides of the filly, she retrieved the saddle from the ground. Again she showed it to Wally. The filly ran her soft nose along the seat and then looked up to Jess, snuffling and waggling her lips around, looking for a pocketful of treats.

Jess tossed the saddle up and over her back. Wally waggled her ears backwards and snorted softly, then resumed her search for treats. 'I didn't bring any, Wal,' said Jess apologetically. 'But I'll get you some after lunch, how does that sound?' She reached under the horse's belly for the girth, pulled it up to the straps and gently eased it onto the third hole, then took a step back and looked at Wally's face.

The filly seemed bored.

'Don't s'pose you've done that before?' asked Luke. His arms were folded and one long leg was crossed over the other as he leaned against the skewbald. He had a suspicious look on his face.

Jess laughed. 'I haven't, I promise. She's just ready, that's all. I could have done this months ago.' She picked up the lead rope and swung the tail of it at Wally's rump. 'Move around, girl, that's it,' she said as the filly moved her hindquarters away from the rope. Jess gently pulled her around and led her out in a spiral. Wally walked happily behind her, occasionally turning and looking at the thing on her back. Jess tightened the girth then led the filly away again, letting her feel it around her belly as she walked.

'Want me to take her for a quick lead off the skewy?' asked Luke.

'Yeah, good idea,' said Jess.

He mounted the skewbald, took Wally's rope, and clicked them both up into a walk. Then he trotted the two horses out in a big circle before returning to Jess. 'Seems pretty quiet.'

Jess led the filly away and found a spot with no trees

or rocks on the ground that might hurt if she landed on them unexpectedly. She lifted the saddle flap and gave the girth one last yank, looked at Wally and hesitated.

'Bring her nose around and yield her hindquarters,' said Luke. 'A horse can't buck while its hind feet are crossing over.'

Jess flexed the filly's neck gently around til her soft nose touched her girth, and then asked her to move her back feet across. 'This is easy, isn't it, Wal?' she said, and repeated it on the other side.

Jess put a foot into the stirrup and sprang lightly onto Wally's back. The filly stood calmly. 'Good girl,' Jess said, turning her in a few small circles. She looked up at Luke. 'Right, let's go count the cattle out.'

Luke looked at his watch. 'We've still got ten minutes.' He lifted his reins and walked his horse on.

Jess clicked up Wally, who followed the skewbald with a swish of her tail. Jess saw Lawson rummaging around in the ute, and couldn't help herself. She rode casually past. 'Got your horse ready, or what?'

He looked up and stalled momentarily, running his eyes over the saddle, the reins, the filly, Jess. He frowned. Behind him, she saw Lindy stifle a grin.

Jess looked at her watch. 'Nine minutes. You're cutting it a bit fine, aren't you?' She clicked Wally up into a slow jog and headed for the cattle.

24

LINDY GOT MOUNTED and yelled instructions while Rosie and Shara let out the cattle. 'String 'em out slowly, girls,' she shouted, then trotted over to Jess and Luke.

'You guys take the eastern side, watch out for open gates and places where the cattle can stray. Keep your distance and keep them quiet. Let 'em graze, then move on a bit.' She pointed at Jess. 'If you have any trouble on that young horse, or if you feel she's had enough, you get straight off her, okay?'

Jess nodded.

Lindy turned her attention back to the throng of mooing and crooning cattle, who were bustling up against each other, impatient to get out. Rosie and Shara made approach-and-retreat movements on their horses, letting them dribble out in small mobs. 'Let 'em fan out,' she called.

'Come this way, Jess.' Luke turned his horse and

trotted along the dirt road, and Jess clicked Wally up and followed. He called out, 'You right to canter?'

'Only one way to find out.' Jess nudged Wally forward and held the front of the saddle with one hand. The filly lurched abruptly into a frolicking, pig-rooting canter. 'Whoa!' The filly's legs felt all tangled. Jess clicked and nudged her into a more forward stride.

Luke looked back. 'You right?'

'Keep going,' she called.

They cantered until they reached the trees about half a kilometre away, where Luke pulled his horse down to a walk. He waited for Jess to ride Wal up beside him. 'She's going great,' he said.

'I knew she would,' Jess beamed.

She saw his eyes run over her and then Wally. 'Shame you never got to own her. She suits you.'

Jess stroked Wally's neck. 'Lawson might own her, but she'll always be *my* buddy.'

'D'you reckon Wally will be all right on her own now?'

'Yeah, fine.'

'Work out wide or they'll bunch up,' said Luke, getting back to work. 'We want them to fan right out and graze. Just keep them headed in the right direction.'

'What about any stragglers?'

'As soon as they see you, they'll go back to the herd anyway. Don't try to chase them on her, will you?'

'Promise.' Jess set off along the fenceline, staying a distance from the cattle.

The morning was hot and long, without incident. Luke rode some distance away from her, arcing back and forth around the tail-end of the cattle. She could hear him singing loudly and shamelessly. Jess remembered the quiet, broody Luke she had first met more than two years ago. He was so different when he was out here.

She was, too. Something about the big space out here let her soul breathe.

When the cattle were settled and grazing, Luke rode over to her. 'I'm going to go and fix up a fence – coming?'

Together they pushed at an old fallen post and pulled the scraps of rusted wire away from it. Luke jammed a strainer post under it and pulled some pliers out of his saddlebag. Jess twisted the top strand back onto itself and tightened the wire by turning it on a stick, the way Rosie had once showed her. Luke used his foot to ram the strainer hard up against the fencepost to keep the whole arrangement tight. When he finished, he looked around at Jess.

He smiled. 'You're just totally meant for me.'

She stood there staring at him, his bare arms hanging from his faded blue shirt, his neck, lean and brown, his throat swallowing and his face, open and somehow completely vulnerable.

He looked down, suddenly shy, and turned back to his horse. 'Better keep an eye on the cattle, I s'pose.' He reached for his stirrup.

She reached out and took hold of his shirt. 'Where are you going?'

He stood still.

Jess pulled him around. 'What's wrong?'

Luke looked to the distance, avoiding her eyes. 'I'm not used to this, I s'pose.' He looked suddenly confused.

'Used to what?' She looked at him with an equal measure of confusion.

He looked down at her, laughed suddenly and put his hands around her neck, pulling her close and pushed his nose into her ear. 'Sorry. I'm an idiot,' he said.

'You are.' Jess put her arms around him. He squeezed her tight and she stood relishing the soft worn fabric of his shirt against her cheek and his chest rising and falling beneath it. She could have stayed like that for hours.

'Cattle are wandering,' he murmured into her hair.

'Mongrel things,' she whispered back.

By noon Wally was beginning to tire, and Jess knew she felt in need of a drink and a rest. The aroma of Mrs Arnold's cooking bread wafted for miles, reaching Jess a good half-hour before she could see the trailer and the ute, and setting her belly rumbling. The cattle seemed to smell it too – Jess could have sworn they ambled in that direction of their own accord.

At a large shaded reserve, Jess and Luke let the cattle stop walking and drop to their bellies beneath the trees. They knew the routine.

Jess dismounted and gave Wally a rub on the neck. 'Good girl,' she said, leading her to some shade. 'I knew you could do it.' She looked into the filly's eyes and saw her own reflection. 'You'll always be my buddy, won't you, girl?' Wally rubbed her face on Jess's arm, begging her to take off the bridle.

As Jess began tying her to a tree, Lawson called, 'Leave her saddled for a minute.' He was unsaddling Chocky by the ute.

Jess let go of the girth straps that she was about to unbuckle. 'She's really tired.'

'I won't do much, just a quick ride.' Lawson gave her a good-natured frown. 'She is *my* filly, you know, and you're doing all the fun bits.'

He came over and took the reins from Jess, then swung up into the saddle. Wally walked off dutifully after a moment of reluctance and gratefully stopped when Lawson leaned back a little in the saddle. He turned her about a couple of times, asked her to trot a circle in each direction, then pulled her back to a halt.

He dismounted, yanked the girth undone and pulled the saddle from Wally's back. 'Nice job, Jess,' he said, sounding impressed. 'She's going real soft.'

'Thanks,' said Jess, taking the saddle from him. She swallowed her pride. 'And thanks for letting me ride her. I knew she was ready.'

'Give her a good rub down and take her back to Bob,' Lawson instructed. He gave Wally a slap on the shoulder and walked away.

She called after him. 'Lawson, wait!'

He stopped and she ran after him. 'Have you heard from the station about Opal?'

Lawson's face softened and Jess instantly felt a wave of nausea rise up from within her. She knew that look. 'What? Is it bad?'

He half-shrugged. 'She's not worse and she's not better. There's a vet that does regular stops in the area and he dropped in and looked at her yesterday. He couldn't find anything either. But she's just—' he hesitated. 'Well, she nearly killed the vet. Opal's not right in the head, Jess. She's dangerous.'

'But Mrs Arnold managed to hook up with her.'

Lawson gave her a rare look of sympathy that made her want to hit him.

No. Don't look at me like that.

She pulled herself together. Getting angry at Lawson, she had learned, got her nowhere. 'Are you still going to let her out onto the station?'

'I don't know.'

Jess took a deep breath. 'Thanks, Lawson,' she said. 'For getting the vet, for not letting her go yet. I know you're trying to look after her,' she paused, 'and me.'

He nodded.

She turned back to Wally and led her away.

'Hey, Jess,' said Lawson.

She spun around.

'Ride Marnie this arvo, hey?'

'Here, take this over to your boyfriend,' Mrs Arnold told Jess, holding a large plate of bread and meat out to her. 'He never bloody stops, that kid.'

She was right. Luke never stopped. Jess felt totally wrecked after six hours in the saddle in the hot sun, while he was using his lunchbreak to shoe horses.

She filled a one-litre water bottle from the tank and took it over to Luke with the plate of food. He was busily filing Wally's hind foot.

'Are you gonna have some lunch?'

'Yep, thanks,' he said. 'Nearly done, just put it on the ground there.'

Jess could see sweat rolling off his temples. The whole back of his shirt was soaked. She twisted the lid off the water bottle and held it over his neck, letting it trickle onto his skin and run down between his shoulder blades.

He stood up and took the bottle from her, draining it in one long guzzle and blissfully inhaling a lungful of air. 'You're so beautiful,' he said, as he wiped his face along his arm.

Jess couldn't even begin to believe how beautiful *he* was right then. His skin was golden from the sun and the dust, and his wet shirt clung to every contour of his shoulders and chest.

He reached for the sandwich. 'Thanks.'

'Wish I had some tomato or something fresh to go with it, but it's all gone,' she said, slightly breathless. 'We'll all get scurvy.'

He tells me I'm beautiful and I start talking about scurvy?

'No asparagus?' he said, taking another hungry bite.

She laughed. 'You're the only other person I know who eats asparagus.'

'You're the only person I know who grows it.'

'It's good for your heart, apparently, and it stops you getting cancer.'

'You're good for my heart,' he said matter-of-factly, seating himself on the ground to finish his lunch.

She smiled and sat next to him. 'Hey, guess what! Lawson told me to ride Marnie this afternoon.'

'Marnie?' He finished one sandwich and grabbed another. 'Wow, he never lets anyone ride her. Do you know how much that horse is worth?'

'Yeah. Hope I don't break her.'

'That'll be like looking into the future – it'll give you an idea of how Opal might turn out.' He paused. 'Have you heard from the homestead? How *is* Opal?'

'Doesn't sound good,' she answered quietly. 'Maybe I should just let her go.'

'Nah. Don't give up on her.'

'I shouldn't let her suffer. She must be in pain, to be behaving like that.'

Luke took the last bite of his sandwich and ran the back of his hand up and down her bare arm.

'You're gonna make me cry doing that,' she warned him.

He ran his hand down to her hand and played with her fingertips, saying nothing.

'Are you gonna come back over to the trailer for a while?' she asked.

'Nah, got two more horses to shoe. I could do them tonight or tomorrow, but I'd rather get it done now so I can hang out tonight. It's our last day out here. We'll reach the saleyards tomorrow.' He held his plate up hopefully. 'Wouldn't mind another sanger, though?'

'Sure,' she said, taking it from him. 'Want another drink?'

He stood up and stretched his legs. 'Thanks.' He held out his hands and pulled her up.

She was in his arms again and he was kissing her. She didn't want it to stop, ever.

25

MARNIE JUMPED SIDEWAYS and snorted at Jess when she tried to pull the girth up. Jess let it fall from her hand and kept hold of the mare's head while the saddle tumbled to the ground. She bent over, picked it up with one hand and somehow shuffled it back onto her arm. 'Whoa, Marnie,' she said quietly, walking after her.

Lawson leaned smirking against the ute, arms folded over his chest. 'She's a cold-backed mare; fine once you get her going, just doesn't like the girth.'

Stan, Ryan, Lindy, Mrs Arnold and Luke all stood alongside him watching. Jess glanced over to the trailer. Shara, Grace and Rosie were looking on as well.

'What, am I today's entertainment or something?' She looked over to the horse break and saw Bob leaning on a tree, observing from a distance. 'Yes, I think I am.'

'Got a good-quality helmet?' Stan called out.

'Why? Am I gonna need it or something?'

Stan just grinned and shrugged, making Jess feel even more suspicious.

She looked anxiously to Luke. He winked at her, which didn't do much to reassure her.

Jess decided to ignore them. She pulled Marnie back towards her and started again, rubbing her neck as she placed the saddle on her back. The mare stood quietly enough. Jess gently pulled her nose around to her belly and held it there. Marnie fidgeted, snorting some more.

'Easy, girl,' said Jess. 'You be nice to me and I'll be nice to you, okay?' She eased up the girth slowly. Marnie stood as still as a statue.

Jess looked at her big, soft eyes. She breathed a sigh of relief and let the mare's head go.

Marnie instantaneously erupted, leaping off the ground into an explosive bucking episode. She reefed the reins through Jess's hands, pulling her off-balance and making her stumble forward.

Jess managed to keep hold of one rein while the mare stuck her head between her knees, brought all four legs off the ground and hammered out another couple of bucks. Jess heard Lawson howl with laughter, while Stan yelled out, 'Bring her head around!'

'Don't let go of my good mare,' Lawson yelled and hooted with laughter again.

Jess held on for another few big humps before she

managed to get her other hand on the reins and plant her feet into the ground. She then pulled sharply at the mare's head, yanking her sideways and off balance, the way Harry had taught her. The reins ran through Jess's grasp and the buckle on the end ripped a chunk of skin off one of her fingers. Marnie came to an abrupt stop and stood with her tail clamped firmly between her legs and her back bent upwards like a banana.

Jess shook her hand and flicked blood onto the ground, mouthing a word that would have earned her a fortnight's grounding from her parents back home.

'You okay?' Luke called out.

'Fine.' Jess glared at Lawson. 'Is she gonna do that again?'

He held up his hands and shrugged, grinning.

Jess put both hands back on the reins and pulled the mare abruptly to the side, bringing her off balance again. She walked around to the other side and gave Marnie another big tug, pulling her off her feet once more. When the mare stood still and loosened her tail a bit, Jess walked towards her hindquarters and waved an arm at her rump. Marnie moved around her in a tight circle, mostly trotting with just a few bunny hops.

'One more time, girl,' she said. 'And don't look at me with those big doe eyes!' She held the horse's nose tight this time and pulled the girth up good and firm. Then she pushed Marnie's hindquarters around and got her feet moving before slowly letting her out into a bigger circle. 'Steady,' she soothed.

Marnie walked around her calmly. Jess led her out into a bigger circle, looked at Lawson and poked her tongue out.

'You haven't got on her yet!' he called out.

Luke reached into the ute and tossed her a helmet.

'Thanks,' Jess said shortly. She buckled it firmly onto her head and looked at her audience. Everyone was still watching – even more intently than before, it seemed.

She jammed Marnie's nose into her ribs, grabbed a stirrup and swung her leg over. Without mucking about, she kicked Marnie into a tight circle, trotting her for a couple of rounds, then swung her back the other way, clicking and clucking, kicking her sides and keeping her feet active. She trotted her out into a bigger circle and changed direction a few more times.

Then she glared at Lawson. 'Show's over.'

He pulled himself off the ute, looking mildly disappointed.

Marnie was like no other horse Jess had ever ridden. She was big, muscular and bouncy – supple and athletic with powerful movement, yet soft, so light she would respond to a feather's touch. The mare made Jess feel as though she were in a boat at sea, rocking gently and rhythmically, but with the power of the ocean beneath her.

Lawson rode up beside her on Slinger. 'Like her?'

'She's beautiful,' Jess gushed.

'Take her for a canter,' he said. 'Try some spins.'

He was gloating, she knew, but Jess wasn't going to argue. She put one leg behind the girth and the mare popped from a walk straight into a steady canter. She brought her seat down in the saddle and the mare slid to a halt with such grace and ease, Jess hardly felt it.

'Roll her back,' Lawson called out.

She barely looked to the left, and Marnie sucked back and spun about in a 180-degree turn, straight into a canter. Jess pushed her out a bit faster and slid her to a halt again, reined her about and galloped off. With the touch of the rein on her neck, and the slight shift of Jess's seat, the mare changed lead legs, then three strides later, changed again. Jess brought her back to a walk and side-passed her across the open country, halted, then side-passed the other way. Marnie was like putty in her hands.

'Take her for a spin,' said Lawson.

Jess halted the mare and looked at him blankly.

'Ask with the outside rein,' he said, holding a rein against Slinger's neck. 'Show with the inside rein.' He opened his other hand out and clucked. Slinger planted one hind foot and pivoted around on his hindquarters for 360 degrees, stopping abruptly to face Jess again.

Jess copied him and laughed out loud as Marnie spun about on her hind foot for three rotations before she asked the mare to stop.

'Other way,' laughed Lawson.

She reined Marnie in the other direction and squealed with delight as the mare spun about.

Lawson winked at her. 'Come on, let's move some cattle.'

Jess moved Marnie off at a walk, smiling from ear to ear.

The others were all saddled and Mrs Arnold was putting up the tailgate of the trailer. Luke waved as he headed off to the east with Grace.

Lawson rode with Jess for a bit and told her how cattle like to walk into the wind so they can smell predators, and showed her how to ride back and forth in big, sweeping arcs to keep them moving steady and calm. Lawson let Jess canter after the strays and bring them back to the herd. After four hours on Marnie's back, Jess felt charged, alive, addicted, fixed.

As they let the last small mob onto the bore to drink late that afternoon, Lawson rode up beside her. 'You know, Jess, if that filly of yours doesn't make it, we could always embryo this one,' he offered, nodding at Marnie.

'You can have another foal from her, even to Biyanga if you want. ET's expensive but you could pay it off by breaking in some horses for me.'

'ET?'

'Embryonic transfer; put her embryo into a donor mare so Marnie doesn't have to be out of work,' he explained. 'Have a think about it.'

As Jess unsaddled Opal's mother at the end of the day, she couldn't help thinking of her filly, lying listlessly in the station yard. Lawson's offer was generous, but she didn't want a new version of Marnie. She wanted Opal.

She couldn't let her die.

26

THAT EVENING, as Jess rummaged in the back of the trailer, looking for something clean to change into, Shara banged on the door. 'Come on, Jess. We're giving you a belated birthday party!'

Jess pulled on a Craig Fairley special, rolled up the roomy sleeves and tied the front shirt tails into a knot. 'I'm coming,' she said, opening the door and jumping out. Lawson was playing some bluegrass tune that filled her with the urge to do some boot scootin' and thigh slappin'.

Shara carried the 'cake' – a large damper – on a plate. In the middle she had shoved a camping candle that was ten times the size of a regular birthday candle. 'Blow it out and make a wish,' said Shara.

'Just one?'

'How many do you need?' asked Shara.

'I have two,' said Jess.

'Rosieee!' Shara yelled. 'Get some more candles. The

birthday queen wants *multiple* wishes.' She lowered her voice to Jess. 'Considering the state of this cake, I think that's a reasonable request!'

'It looks delicious,' said Jess.

'Made by my own fair hand,' said Shara proudly.

Rosie came over with some more white candles and shoved them unceremoniously into the crust of the damper. 'Who's got a match?'

'Here.' Grace held a stick in the fire and caught some flame, then lit the candles one by one. 'Happy birthday to you,' she began to sing and the others joined in for another round of the song.

'Make your wishes,' said Shara.

Jess blew from candle to candle until they were all extinguished.

I wish Opal gets better.

I wish these guys are my friends forever and ever.

As plates of warm damper with butter and golden syrup were passed around, Shara sidled up to her. 'So, best bestie,' she said, in a secretive whisper. 'We all want to know what's going on with Luke.' She nudged Jess.

'We saw you kissing,' teased Rosie as she sat down next to them. 'Told you he was totally in love with you.'

'Gross, I'm never having a boyfriend,' said Grace, tearing open her chunk of damper and watching the steam come out.

Jess smirked and took a bite of her damper without answering. 'This is disgusting!' She searched for somewhere to spit out her mouthful.

Shara spat hers onto her plate. 'I think I used salt instead of sugar!' she moaned.

That night, Stan showed Jess how to play a few chords on a guitar.

'I think I have two left hands,' she said, picking up her index finger with her other hand and forcing it back down to where it was supposed to be. Her fingers were as stiff as pencils, seemingly severed from any connection with her brain. Maybe if she stared at them a bit harder they might do as they were told.

Stan plucked clumsily at Harry's banjo, pausing to adjust at each chord change. 'Yeah, can't say I was born with any real talent either,' he said. 'Not like them Blake boys.'

Jess found the G chord and triumphantly hammered the strings. 'Dah nahhh!' she sang.

'Ah, you've got the voice of an angel,' said Stan, sounding pleased for her. 'Nearly brings a tear to me eye.'

'It's bringing a tear to my *ear*,' said Ryan from the

other side of the fire. He walked over and held out his hand for the guitar. 'Mind?'

Jess gladly handed it over.

'Oi, *Luke*!' Lawson yelled, loud enough to make Jess jump. 'Stop working and get over here.'

'I'm packing up the horse gear,' Luke called.

'Do it tomorrow!'

'Nearly done,' Luke called back. 'Legs lost a shoe. Just gonna peg it back on.'

Lawson groaned and pulled himself up off the ground. 'I'll do the horse, you get the gear.'

Lindy sat next to Jess with a bowl of steaming lamb stew. She took a mouthful and as she chewed, she looked over to the ute where Lawson and Luke worked alongside each other in the dimming orange light. She sighed. 'What is it about farriers, Jess? I never met an ugly one.'

Jess looked at Lawson bent over under the horse. 'That's because you never look at their heads.'

Within a few minutes, Lawson and Luke walked back to the campfire. Lawson squatted down next to Jess. 'I was just talking to Luke. There are some more youngsters back home you can break in next holidays if you want,' he said. 'Earn some pocket money. You and Luke can work together. You make a good team.'

Luke looked at her and grinned.

'Okay.' Jess beamed. The next holidays were the Christmas holidays; six whole weeks of Luke and horses. She couldn't *wait*!

Lawson turned to Stan, who was still playing the same three chords over and over. 'Better give me that thing before you spook the cattle.'

Stan held it out to him. 'Me fingers are bleeding anyway.'

Luke plonked himself behind Jess and wrapped his arms around her waist. 'I'm stuffed.'

'I was beginning to wonder if you *ever* got tired,' she said, leaning her head back into him. She stared into the fire. Its tongues lashed greedily around the dry mulga timber and rose tall into the windless evening.

'What was Marnie like to ride?'

'Like a six-hundred-kilo ballerina.'

A wave of blinding light flashed over the trailer and there was an uproarious whining and howling that set off every other dog in the camp.

'Who's that?' Grace asked, shielding her eyes with her arm.

Jess heard Luke laugh behind her. He gently pushed her forward and then stood up and whistled.

Two dark shapes, howling and barking, came barrelling into the fireside light and launched themselves onto Luke, sending him staggering backwards and onto his bum. 'Hey buddies,' he yelled, as he rolled around with Filth and Fang, laughing. The dogs growled and whined playfully.

'Filth!' Luke screamed as the black dog mouthed his arm and shook it playfully. 'Gentle!'

The lights flashed over them again and the sound of a car's tyres rumbled along the ground. A horn honked.

Luke stood and took the two dogs by the collars, struggling to hold them. 'It's Tom!' He squinted into the lights. 'And someone else.'

Jess felt a hand on her shoulder and spun around. Grace stared back at her with a look of utter panic.

'Jess, quick,' Grace hissed, motioning for her to follow.

'What's wrong?' Jess asked, as Grace pulled at her sleeve. 'Hey, watch the flannie!'

Grace kept tugging. 'Pleeease,' she moaned.

Jess heard Tom's voice as he got out of the car.

'I had to bring the dogs out,' he said. 'They were driving Annie nuts, howling all night.'

'I'd given up on you,' said Luke, throwing his arms around Tom's neck and jumping all over him. 'Thought you weren't coming.'

Tom pushed him off and soon they were wrestling like two puppies, with Filth and Fang leaping on top to join in.

'That is just a little *too Brokeback Mountain*,' said Jess.

'No, it's not,' said Grace, dragging Jess towards and into the trailer.

'What is *wrong*?' asked Jess. She'd never seen Grace so het up.

Grace made pointing gestures out the door and opened her eyes wide, making Jess guess.

Jess held her hands up, making her face vacant and questioning.

Grace screwed her nose up with frustration. 'Elliot's here,' she spat, like an annoyed cat.

'So?'

Grace rolled her eyes and sighed an agonised sigh.

'Ohhh . . . *Elliot*,' said Jess. 'And?' She looked at Grace. 'Oh my God, you kissed him!'

Grace nodded, wincing.

Jess threw her hands over her mouth and caught an enormous barrel of laughter before it escaped from her throat. 'How did that happen?' she whispered. 'I thought you hated boys!'

'It happened just before we came out here. I was going to tell you but he said he was coming droving and then he didn't come and then . . . I was beginning to think it never happened.'

They stared at each other, hands over their mouths.

'Elliot?' Jess marvelled. She still couldn't believe it – Grace and the super geek. She stifled another laugh.

'What's so funny?' Grace hissed. 'You and Luke have been at it all day!'

'Nothing. Nothing's funny. Does Rosie know?'

'Of course not!'

Jess broke out laughing. Rosie would be merciless when she found out.

Grace began frantically rummaging through the whiffy rags strewn over the bunk. 'I need some clean clothes.'

'You've got no hope,' said Jess.

'Look at me,' Grace moaned. She was wearing a pair of old trackpants that had holes in the knees, with a Craig Fairley special on top. '*He* looks like someone out of an IT magazine.'

'I've got some cut-off jeans that are still clean.'

'Shorts?'

'Sure, come here.' Jess patted her hands over Grace's hips and then her bum. 'Hmmm . . .'

'Now who's *Brokeback Mountain*?' said Grace impatiently.

'We need Rosie,' said Jess.

'No way.'

'She's your only hope.'

'*No!*'

'Yes!'

Jess leapt out of the trailer. Beyond the fire, Luke and Tom were trying to take down Lawson, who rambled about like King Kong with two monkeys clinging to him, two wolves growling at his heels. A body went sailing across the shadows and into a tree; she wasn't sure if it was Luke or Tom. She ran around to the water tanks on the back of the truck and found Rosie with her hair wrapped in a towel, brushing her teeth into a bucket.

She pulled her brush from her mouth when she saw Jess. 'Whose car was that?'

'Rosie!' Jess grabbed her by the arm and began dragging her into the trailer. 'Huge crisis, in the trailer, quick!'

'Hey!' said Rosie, 'at least let me rinse!'

'No time,' said Jess, pulling her along. 'Grace needs a big sister!'

Within fifteen minutes, through quick explanations, gasps and whispered tell-alls, Rosie had Grace into a pair of clean jeans, pilfered from the washing nets in the back of the truck, a skin-tight black cotton singlet and one of Lindy's country-brand caps with a ponytail poking out the back. She was sponged, deodorised, cleansed and toned. Her teeth were brushed and her toenails painted – they decided bare feet would look casually confident, girly and earthy. Men found feet sexy, Rosie assured them, especially with painted toenails. She had read about it in a magazine.

'As if he's even gonna see my feet,' complained Grace. 'It's dark!'

'Don't be such a sad loser,' said Rosie, applying a second coating of polish. She was in her element. 'Do you want to look hot or not?'

Rosie screwed the lid back on the bottle and pulled Grace up onto her feet.

Jess let out a long, breezy wolfwhistle. 'Nice work, Rosie!'

With her tanned skin, blonde hair and dark eyes, Grace was absolutely gorgeous.

'One more thing,' said Rosie, reaching into her make-up bag and pulling out some lip gloss. 'Strawberry or caramel?'

'He strikes me as more of the Juicyfruit type,' Shara commented from the top bunk.

'Oh no,' Grace groaned.

'Go for the strawberry,' said Jess quickly. 'It's high in vitamin C . . . and anti-oxidants.'

Grace screwed up her face at her.

Jess shrugged. 'You don't want spongy gums and bleeding teeth when you're kissing a guy, believe me.'

'What?' said Rosie, looking disgusted.

'Nothing, forget it.'

Grace smiled nervously. 'Do I look okay?'

'More than okay,' said Jess, shoving her towards the doorway. 'Don't you go near Luke looking like that,' she teased.

'Look at your boobs,' said Rosie. 'When did they happen?'

Grace immediately reached for the flannie.

'No way,' said Rosie, snatching it and shoving Grace towards the door. 'Now, go get him.'

Grace stumbled out of the trailer and into the dim lamp over the trailer door, Jess and Rosie close behind her. On the other side of the fire, Lawson, Luke and Tom walked back to the camp, talking and laughing loudly. They all saw Grace at the same time and shut up.

'Err, hi,' said Grace, turning and trying to step back into the trailer. Rosie and Jess blocked her path and not-very-subtly herded her towards the fire. Elliot sat neatly on a tree stump, blinking through his glasses at something electronic and beeping in his hands.

'Hi, Elliot,' said Rosie loudly.

'Hi,' said Elliot, without lifting his eyes.

'Good drive out here?'

'Ummm . . . yes.'

Rosie shoved Grace at him. Grace pushed her off. 'Okay, okay.' She sat down next to him, looking grumpy.

'They're making me sit next to you,' she said with her arms folded, staring away from him.

'I know,' Elliott said, without looking up from his gadget.

'Hi, Rosie!' It was Tom.

Rosie spun around. 'Oh my God, my hair's not done!' she shrieked and raced back into the trailer, leaving him looking confused.

King Kong came back from the wilds of the water trough and scooped Lindy into his arms, dancing around the fire with her.

Luke looked across the camp, first at Grace and Elliot, then at Lawson and Lindy, then at Tom hovering outside the trailer door. 'Have I missed something?'

Stan started whistling 'Love Is in the Air', walked over to Mrs Arnold and tried to put his arm around her waist. She raised her frying pan at him. 'Bugger off, Stan.'

'Oh, come on, old girl, you used to love dancing.'

Mrs Arnold dropped her pan and rolled her eyes.

'Woohoo!' said Rosie, as she stepped out of the trailer, reinvented, and saw her parents dancing. 'Go for it, big daddy-o!'

Stan lifted an arm above his wife's head and sent her into a twirl.

'Let's drink a toast to Harry,' said Lawson.

The whole campsite came to a screaming halt. The Arnolds stopped dancing, the music stopped and everybody glared at Lawson.

'What?' said Lawson. 'It's a good and proper use for alcohol.'

'And cooking's not?' said Mrs Arnold, incredulous.

'Not if you don't hide it properly.' He grinned and pulled a small clay bottle from the dogbox in the trailer. 'Find a mug.'

'The bloody hide of it,' said Mrs Arnold.

It was only a small bottle, and it was by no means full, but Lawson managed to deal a dribble into each mug. Ryan politely declined, filling his cup instead with some hot coffee. They raised their odd assortment of plastic, tin and aluminium cups and banged them all together, celebrating the man who had brought them all there together like a big family, bonded by the horses, the cattle, the dust and the liquid that burned down their throats.

A breeze blew over the fire, sending sparks into the air like little fireworks. It blew the hair up off Jess's neck.

Here's to you, Harry.

She sat by the fire, snuggled into Luke's lap, dogs by her feet, listening to the soft guitar, the crickets, the cattle, smelling smoke and eucalyptus, watching the fire and the faces of her friends glowing around it. She couldn't remember feeling more happy and alive.

Luke's fingers ran absent-mindedly up and down her arm and in soft little circles. His chest rose slowly with each breath. Jess closed her eyes and breathed in time with him, letting his body rock her gently to sleep.

27

THE NEXT MORNING, Jess flipped some eggs over, gave them a quick shake around the pan and tipped them onto Lindy's plate.

'Will you come and see us at Coachwood Crossing, Lindy?' she asked.

'Sure will, it sounds beautiful,' answered Lindy. 'Just gotta get these cattle through the sales and sort out a few things at home. What's up ahead for you?

'School.' Jess cracked some more eggs into the pan. 'I'm a bit of a nerd, really, but don't tell anyone.'

'Good girl,' said Lindy. 'I spent four years at uni – best thing I ever did.' She grabbed a chunk of bread off the table and poured tomato sauce over her eggs. 'If you want some holiday work at Longwood, come and see me, hey?'

'Sure, thanks,' said Jess.

Lindy nodded over towards the ute. Three lanky pairs of legs – Tom's, Elliot's and Luke's – hung out of the open bonnet. It looked like an old yellow dinosaur getting its teeth done, especially next to Tom's late-model sleek black Holden. 'I gave Luke that old ute. He's in heaven.' As Lindy walked away, she said, 'Sorry, Jess, but there's another woman in his life now.'

Luke pulled his head out from under the bonnet and turned around, looking for Jess. He waved her over, his grin so wide it nearly split his head in half. 'Come and look,' he said excitedly. 'It's a 1973 HQ, totally original. It even has a miles-per-hour speedo!'

He leaned into the cabin. 'The cigarette lighter still works!'

'Great, I can charge my mobile,' said Jess.

Luke poked his head back out, frowned briefly, then grinned again. 'I can't believe it's mine! Lindy gave it to me for wages.'

'He would've loved you to have it.' Jess stuck her head in the cabin. 'Shame the seats are all ripped.'

'Yeah, but they're *bench* seats.' Luke beamed, and Jess wondered why that was so good. 'I'll fix 'em up and put covers over them. I'll get her looking like new.' He ran his hand lovingly over the cracked dashboard. 'Come and see under the bonnet,' he said, dragging her around to the front.

Tom was up to his armpits in the car's gizzards. 'Think she needs uni joints. Rats've chewed holes in the washer bottle,' he said without raising his head.

'Most of this stuff's computerised these days,' said Elliot.

Jess listened to them talk excitedly about car bits that she'd never heard of until she eventually tuned out and found herself ogling Luke's strong forearms under his rolled-up sleeves.

He is so gorgeous and he is so mine.

He turned to her suddenly. 'Let's go driving out west for a few days. Lawson doesn't need me once we get the cattle into the saleyards, and TAFE's not back for another week.'

Jess immediately imagined sitting in the front of the ute with Luke, talking and laughing, and watching the endless mulga country float by. Camping in swags under the stars and kissing him endlessly. She was more than tempted, but reality broke back in. 'I can't.'

'Why not?'

'I have to go back and see Opal,' she said. 'I need to sort her out, one way or the other.'

He put his arms around her and sighed a frustrated sigh. 'But I want you all to myself.'

'I've also got school and parents who would totally freak.'

'Oh yeah, I forget about that sort of thing.'

Jess put her arms around his waist. They had been

together only days and yet she couldn't imagine being away from him ever again. Out here she was a part of his day-to-day life; they ate every meal together. They were wild and free – except for Mrs Arnold. Back home he would work all day while she was at school. He would seem like such an adult, and she would feel like such a schoolkid.

'I'll drive you back to the station.'

'No, you won't,' said Mrs Arnold, walking up behind them with the large frying pan in her hand.

Jess and Luke both groaned.

Later that afternoon, the cattle were in a holding paddock near the saleyards, and the entire droving outfit was packed up and ready to head back to Blakely Downs. Luke was still messing about under the bonnet of the ute with Tom, topping up oil and water. Being unregistered, he planned to drive back along the stock route to the station, deeming the lack of a driver's side door to be too much of a 'cop magnet' to take it on the highway. Elliot sat in the passenger seat of Tom's ute, quietly thumbing away at his beeping gadget while he waited.

Jess climbed into the back seat of Mrs Arnold's LandCruiser and squeezed in next to Shara.

Mrs Arnold started the engine and rolled slowly towards the gooseneck trailer. The tailgate was down, ready for loading the horses; by the cabin, Stan filled the diesel tanks from jerry cans. Nearby, Bob stood barefoot with five horses in halters behind him, like a bunch of balloons. The cuffs of his jeans were frayed where they dragged on the ground, his gnarly feet so covered in dust it was hard to know where the man ended and the earth began. Lawson took Marnie from him, led her to the ramp and both man and horse disappeared into the back of the trailer for a moment.

Jess leaned out the window. 'See ya, Bob!'

Bob walked towards the four-wheel drive and pulled something out of his pocket. 'Happy birthday, Jessy.'

Jess took the small ball of grimy blue cloth, like a rag cut from an old T-shirt. A piece of string held it closed. She could feel something lumpy inside it.

'Find her spirit, catch it, and take it back to her,' Bob said softly.

'Thanks,' she said, staring at the bundle in her hands.

'You let me know when you wanna sell that old stockhorse.'

Jess smiled. 'You'll be waiting a while.'

'See you back at the station, ay.'

Mrs Arnold let the brake off and they began to roll away.

In the car, Jess rolled the rag about in her hands, puzzled.

'What is it?' asked Shara, nodding at the small bundle. 'Open it.'

Jess began to pick at the string until it slipped over the rag and fell away. Then she unrolled it. Inside was a short stump of mulga wood shaped like a horse. A lumpy knot in the timber created the shape of the shoulder perfectly and, from that, the branch arched into a neck. Where the stick had snapped off the tree, the splintered timber formed the shape of two ears and a horse's head.

She turned it over, ran her finger along the neck and touched three teeny-weeny diamonds carved into its shoulder.

'Did Bob make that for you?' asked Shara, staring over her shoulder.

'It's Opal,' said Jess, still examining it closely and noticing its long mane, like that of a mature horse rather than a foal. 'He *must* have made it.' She twisted around and looked through the billows of dust behind the car.

Bob fastened the gate. Behind him the low hills rolled away, and the mulga trees shimmered in the unrelenting sun.

Jess pushed the carving into her pocket and pulled out the Yowah nuts.

'Can we stop at a post office, Mrs A?'

An hour or so along the highway, Mrs Arnold pulled into a service station and cut the engine. Jess jumped down to stretch her legs, her friends tumbling out behind her.

'Post office is over the road,' said Mrs Arnold, jabbing her thumb over her shoulder, as she walked to the bowser.

Jess pulled her pack over her shoulder and with the nuts in her hand, ran across the road. Five minutes later, she emerged from the small timber building with a small padded envelope, addressed to David Rawlins, care of Yowah Post Office.

Jess lifted the lid on the postbox, inserted the small parcel and pushed the chute down again. 'Enjoy your bad-luck stones, Dave.' Briskly brushing her hands together, she headed back to the servo.

As she crossed the road, her phone buzzed in her pocket. 'Hey! There must be mobile reception around here,' she said, tearing it out.

'Yep,' said Mrs Arnold, pointing to two satellite towers on a nearby hill as she put the pump handle back onto the bowser.

Jess flipped it open and gasped as she saw it light up in her hand. 'It's back from the dead!'

There were four messages. She leaned against the

four-wheel drive and scrolled through them while the others went into the shop for ice-creams. The first was from the day before.

BDowns: the fillys taken a bad turn, pls contact station.

Jess felt a sudden heaviness as she realised the rest of the messages were not going to be good. She scrolled to the next one with a weighty thumb.

BDowns: ring urgently – need permission.

Twelve hours ago? She's already dead.

Guilt consumed her. She'd been gallivanting around out here while Opal had been dying. She should never have left her.

Jess couldn't help it; she sobbed.

'What? What is it?' asked Shara, coming out of the shop with two ice-creams in her hand. She ran to Jess.

Jess passed her the phone. 'You read the next message. I can't.'

'Is it about Opal?'

Jess nodded and looked down.

'The next one's from your mum. It says *Happy birthday*

darlin, I love you,' said Shara. She kept thumbing. 'Ooh, there's a really mushy one from Luke.'

Jess snatched the mobile.

Luke: jess, i had the best time. C u and O at
the station.

A tear dropped onto the screen. Jess smudged it away with her thumb and wiped her eyes with her sleeve, then scrolled back up to the station's last message and replied.

is she still alive?

She tucked the phone into her top pocket and followed the others into the four-wheel drive. Mrs Arnold took off and Jess looked miserably out the window at the country whipping by. She felt numb, waiting for an answer.

Buzz, rumble.

BDowns: only just.

Jess thumbed back.

we're 1 hour away, pls, pls, pls, wait for me.

28

AT THE HOMESTEAD, Opal lay on the ground, not moving. Her hair was coarse and matted except for some bald bits on her legs and back. She was painfully thin.

Jess let herself in through the yard gate while Shara, Rosie and Grace looked over the rails.

'Vet's been twice and given her IV fluids,' said the stockman, as Jess knelt beside him. 'But it doesn't seem to cure her. She hasn't moved for hours.'

Jess felt sick. She could see death taking over the filly.

Opal rubbed her head along the muddy ground and a tiny groan escaped her throat. Jess cast her eye over her shoulder and there they were – the three white diamonds, cascading like falling stars.

She ran a hand over the filly's neck. It was hot and damp with sweat. Jess put her hand in her pocket, pulled out the carving and remembered Bob's words as she fingered the three diamonds on its shoulder.

Find her spirit, catch it and take it back to her.

'This was meant to be for you,' she whispered, running it over her filly's neck and up around her ears. 'It's your totem, Opal.' Jess couldn't stop the tears that flowed from her. 'You're just a little mulga filly.'

Opal lay still, very still. Jess's whole body began to sink. It was too late. She dropped the carving and sank to the ground, putting her face against the cool earth.

I can't let her go. She's meant to be mine.

Around her the world stood still. She closed her eyes and listened for the spirits that were alive in the land.

Please give my filly life. Don't take her back yet.

She wasn't sure how long she lay there, whispering and praying. Time seemed to stop. A tiny sound made its way to her ears. It wasn't a whinny and it wasn't a cry. Just a little noise: air, vibrating out of black rubbery nostrils. Jess looked up and through her blurred vision, she saw Opal move. The filly's head slid ever so slightly across the ground. Jess got to her hands and knees and crawled quietly to her.

Thick yellow-green pus ran from behind Opal's ear.

Jess's skin prickled. Poison.

She felt a warm breeze, like the breath of a horse, blow down her neck. And then the strangest thing happened.

Opal stood up.

'Kworr, that's gross!' said Grace, from the yard rail. 'It stinks, I can smell it from here!'

'It *is* like a curse,' said Jess, looking at the disgusting goo oozing from Opal's head. She screwed up her face. 'It looks evil.'

'You got that bit right,' said Lawson. 'That's the old-fashioned name for it – Poll Evil.' He reached for an old rag and Jess kept her arm under Opal's neck as he began wiping the pus away. Opal flinched.

'Easy, girl,' said Lawson. 'Bet that's feeling a whole lot better now.'

He turned to Jess. 'In the old days, before vets had antibiotics, it was nearly impossible to treat. The horses got so cranky with pain they became vicious. Most of them had to be destroyed.'

'But we won't have to destroy Opal, will we?' Jess said quickly. 'It can be treated these days, can't it?'

'She'll need an operation to clean it out, but I don't know who's gonna do that around here.' He looked to Stanley. 'You any good on this sort of thing?'

Stan shook his head.

.'I knew there'd be a scientific explanation.' Shara

jumped off the fence and stepped forward. 'One student vet, at your service!'

Luke peered over Lawson's shoulder. 'You need a TMU.'

Lawson and Stan both stared at him blankly.

'That's what they used on me up north.'

'Did it hurt?' asked Stan.

Luke snorted at him. 'A tele-medicine unit! They did it all over the internet. The medicos just told the nurses what to do. We could get John on the phone, text him some photos, then put him on speakerphone while Shara does what he says.' He looked from Stan to Shara.

She nodded in agreement.

'You're a genius, Luke!' said Jess.

Stan looked at Lawson. Lawson shrugged. 'Well, I've got a fridge full of drugs that John sent out here with her.'

'Where's our resident communications expert?' asked Stan.

Elliot stood out in the middle of a nearby yard waving some sort of small hand-held device around and squinting up at the sky.

'He's trying to find a satellite for his GPS,' said Grace. Then she shouted, *'Elliot!'*

'Yeah?' he yelled back, without looking down.

'We need tech support!'

Jess helped gather all the veterinary first aid they could find, and under Elliot's command, they managed to somehow link the satellite phone, a laptop computer and a GPS satellite tracking device, as well as a car battery and a few other bits and bobs. They set it up on the fold-out camp table out in the middle of the yard and Jess watched in wonder as John's face popped up on the computer screen.

'Hi, Dad,' said Elliot, holding the webcam up to his face.

'What's going on out there?' asked John, his voice digitally fragmented.

Behind her, Jess heard Grace's awed whisper to Shara: 'El's *sooo* brainy!'

Elliot held the webcam at Opal's head while John watched the images come through at his end. He told Shara where to squeeze and prod, how to take Opal's temperature and listen to her heart rate. Shara spoke back to him through a set of headphones and a microphone that Elliot had attached to her head.

They took still photos and messaged them, and then John talked Shara through the procedure of flushing the wound with peroxide to clean it out. Stanley hunted through the leftover veterinary drugs the station had on hand and managed to locate some painkillers. John prescribed a dose and instructed Shara through the intravenous injecting.

Jess knelt by Opal's head, talking quietly and supporting her through the ordeal.

As Shara finished up and washed her hands by the trough, John spoke to Jess on the phone. 'I'm so sorry, Jess. It must have been in there brewing for weeks. No wonder she was so wild with pain.'

'I *knew* it wasn't just her temperament,' said Jess.

'Those antibiotics we gave her would have calmed it down, but it obviously didn't get rid of it completely. We didn't know what we were treating then, I suppose.' He paused. 'I can't believe I missed it. There was no outward sign. Usually they have a huge lump on their head.'

'It wasn't your fault,' Jess assured him. 'Will she have to go to a vet hospital again?'

'Yes, she should. Shara's only given her basic first aid. She'll need to be knocked out and operated on properly. The DPI might want to quarantine her for a while too. It's a notifiable disease.'

'Will she travel okay, do you think?'

'Leave her in the yard overnight to stabilise. I've told Shara to keep up with the painkillers, then truck her to the Longwood vet surgery tomorrow morning. I'll ring ahead for you and book her in.'

While the others headed for the house, Jess knelt by

257

Opal's head and stroked her neck. Within minutes the filly began to shuffle to her feet and raise her head. With a snort and a grunt, she lifted herself to a more upright position and blinked at Jess. The two of them stared as though seeing each other for the very first time.

'Hey, little girl. How you feeling?'

Opal closed her eyes briefly, still groggy.

Jess reached into her pocket for a small crust of bread and held it out on the palm of her hand. 'Want some bread? I saved it for you.'

The filly sniffed. She lifted her nose just a little and blinked.

A smile washed over Jess's whole being. 'It's very tasty.'

Opal waggled her lips.

'Come on . . .'

Opal worked her lips like a pair of hands, taking the bread into her mouth. She munched it slowly, an uncertain look in her eye. Her fuzzy chin brushed over Jess's hand. It was exquisitely soft.

'There we go, little one,' Jess smiled. 'You're going to be fine now.'

29

EARLY THE NEXT MORNING, Luke led Rusty onto the float first. 'To keep Opal company,' he explained. 'He's a sensible little fella, he'll help keep her calm.'

Jess led Opal, with a rope looped loosely around her neck, into the trailer beside the little brumby. Lawson lifted the tailgate behind them and Jess tethered the little filly. She looked back at her as she stepped out of the narrow front door. 'Be good,' she said and closed the door.

Lawson leaned out of the driver's side window. 'Do you trust me to get her there in one piece?'

'Not really,' Jess answered. 'I don't know why Mrs Arnold won't let me travel with you.'

Luke jumped in the passenger side door. 'It's because I'm in here! You'll get boy germs.'

'I'm taking him into town to get some parts for that ute,' said Lawson. 'You'll be driving right behind us.'

'Drive carefully.'

'Aren't you forgetting something?' asked Lawson.

'What?'

He smiled. 'You owe me two hundred and forty-six bucks.'

Jess smiled back. 'Not yet.'

'But I want you to pay me for her. She'll be yours.'

'But I have no money now,' said Jess, trying to keep a straight face. 'I spent it all on a Yowah nut,' she lied.

Lawson looked at her, puzzled.

'Won't take me long to save the money again,' she said in a reassuring tone. 'Meanwhile, I guess you're stuck with her . . . and all her vet bills.' She turned on her heel and, smirking, walked back towards Mrs Arnold's four-wheel drive.

She heard Lawson roar with laughter. 'You can have her for free!' he called after her, 'if you take her now! She's all yours!'

'See you at the surgery!' said Jess, walking away.

'Girls and *bloody* horses!' he yelled.

Opal was operated on almost immediately after arriving at the surgery. Shara got talking to the vet nurse and was thrilled to find that she too had gone to Canningdale. Shara and Jess were allowed to sit in on the operation.

Jess watched while the vet scooped gunk out of Opal's head, packed the wound full of iodine-soaked gauze and stitched it up.

They walked outside and sat in the gardens while Opal rested and came to. Luke and Lawson returned from the auto wrecker, triumphant with an HQ Holden door, new tyres and various other miscellaneous car-fixing-type stuff.

Luke sat on the bench seat next to Jess going through bags of bog and putty, talking a million miles an hour about how sleek his ute was going to be. 'How'd Opal go?' he finally asked. 'What are you going to do, stay in Longwood till she gets better?' He sounded hopeful. 'We're staying for another week, until the ute's going and registered. Bob's helping me.'

'I have to go home,' said Jess. 'Mum and Dad won't let me stay any longer.'

'When I get my ute going, I can drive you back out on the weekends to visit her,' promised Luke. He grinned. 'I'll get you all to myself! No Mrs Arnold!'

Jess beamed. No Mrs Arnold; just Luke, Opal and her. 'That would be so good!'

'She's gonna be a great horse, Jess.'

'I reckon she is, too.'

'Gonna have to get going soon, you two,' said Mrs Arnold, appearing from the large red-brick building.

'I told your mum I'd have you home in time to go to school tomorrow.'

'Okay,' said Jess, pulling herself up off the seat. 'Can I run in and say goodbye to Opal first?'

'Yeah, but be quick,' said Mrs Arnold. 'I'll be waiting in the car.'

'Coming?' Jess asked Luke.

He shook his head. 'You go, I gotta get something out of the car, I nearly forgot.'

Jess ran back into the building, through reception and into the recovery area. She found Opal, standing and drinking from the small automatic waterer at the corner of the stable.

'That's a good sign,' said Shara, joining her at the door. She put an arm over Jess's shoulder.

Jess put her arm over Shara's and they stood there watching Opal. 'She's gonna be fine now,' Jess said.

'Yeah, she's on the mend.'

Jess tilted her head and let it rest on Shara's shoulder. 'Thanks, bestie.'

'That's best bestie to you.'

'Best bestie,' Jess corrected herself.

'*Dr* Best Bestie.'

'*Dr* Best Bestie.'

'Dr Best Vet in the World Best Bestie.'

Jess laughed. 'Don't push it.'

'See you back at the car. I'll let you guys say goodbye.'

As Shara walked out of the building, Jess took a last look at Opal and tried to imagine how she would look in two weeks' time, when she'd put some weight on, and in four weeks when her coat would have a shine, and in two years' time as a strong, healthy two-year-old, ready to come home and live with her forever. 'You'll be worth the wait, Opal,' she whispered. Then she turned about. 'See you in a couple of weeks.'

As Jess climbed into Mrs Arnold's LandCruiser, she saw Luke fumbling around in the front of the ute. He got out with a small plastic bag in his hand and ran back over to her. 'Asparagus,' he said, passing it through the car window. 'Got it in town this morning. So you don't get scurvy on the way home.'

I'm gonna marry you one day, Luke Matheson.

'You're so funny,' she laughed.

'Oh my Gawd,' Shara groaned beside her. 'You two are a match made in heaven.'

Luke grinned at Jess, then looked suddenly awkward. 'Can I ask you a favour?'

'Sure.'

'I bought a new horse. She's at Harry's place.'

Jess's face lit up. 'A new horse? When did you buy her?'

'Well, I didn't exactly *buy* her. I adopted her.'

'Adopted her?' Jess heard a cacophony of bells as she realised who Luke was talking about. 'You what?'

'From the RSPCA,' he said. 'I've always liked her.'

Jess looked at him, aghast. 'You *didn't*?'

'I did.'

'What *for*?'

'Chelpie's so well bred. She's got good feet. Lawson and I were thinking she'd be perfect for our breeding program; she'd inject a bit of class into it.'

'*Class*?'

He shrugged.

'*You own Chelpie*?'

'Uhuh.'

'And you want *me* to look after her?'

'Just until I come back, then we'll bring her back out here when we come to visit Opal and let her go with the brumbies.' He gave her a meek smile, his head tilted. 'Please?'

'She's totally nutty, dysfunctional, poorly raised. She's—'

He looked at her with the softest, most totally impossible-to-resist eyes. 'I came good with the right mob, didn't I?'

Jess steeled herself against the melting, giddy, hopelessly weak feeling in her gut. She reined in her smile behind a tight-set mouth. 'One bag of asparagus is not gonna make up for this.'

'I'll buy you a whole farm of asparagus.'

'I already *have* a whole farm of asparagus.'

'Capsicums, then?'

Jess undid her seatbelt, leaned as far as she could out of the window and threw her arms around Luke's neck. His cheek was spiky against her ear. 'Only for you.' She squeezed him and he squeezed her back. The car began to move and he walked with her for a while, holding her tight and threatening to pull her out of the car window.

'I'll look after Opal for you,' he whispered.

'And I'll look after Chelpie,' she laughed, and let him go. She hung out of the window and waved. He stood there, hands in his dirty denim pockets, two big wolf dogs panting either side of him, his ute behind him, and beyond that the endless flat mulga country with its soft curling Mitchell grass and stumpy trees.

Acknowledgements

Many, many thanks to the team at Allen and Unwin: Erica Wagner for 'discovering' my stories and believing in them, Sarah Brenan for shaping them and putting them on track for publication, Hilary Reynolds for being so in tune with my characters and having such perfect suggestions, and Ruth Grüner for the amazing covers and posters – I've loved working with you all.

To Tyson Kaawoppa Yunkaporta, again thanks for contributing to my books with such an open and generous spirit.

To Jody Allen, thanks for the heads-up on droving!

To Dr Keith Phillips, thanks for your advice!

To my perfect husband for his continuing love and support – thanks, Big Daddy-o!

And to the first people of this beautiful country – with all of my heart, I'm sorry.

About the Author

KAREN WOOD has been involved with horses for more than twenty years. After owning many horses, she has finally found her once-in-a-lifetime horse in a little chestnut stockhorse called Reo. Karen has an Arts degree majoring in communications and a diploma in horticulture. She has syndicated a gardening column in several newspapers throughout Australia, has published feature articles in various magazines and has published photographs in bushwalking guides. She is married with two children and lives on the Central Coast, New South Wales.

DIAMOND SPIRIT

A man Jess had never seen before stood holding
the flyscreen door open.
'Do you own an Appaloosa pony?' he asked.
'Yes.'
'It's stuck in the cattle grid down near the old drovers' yards.'
Jess's blood ran cold.

At the start of the summer holidays, the unthinkable happens
when Jess's beloved pony Diamond has a terrible accident.
Why won't Shara, Jess's closest friend, tell her what happened
down on the river flats that day? Jess suspects the worst, and feels
as though she's lost not just one best friend, but two.

But new friends and new horses come into Jess's life,
along with the chance to compete in the Longwood campdraft.
And there's one little filly who needs her help . . . Can Walkabout
heal Jess's broken heart in return?

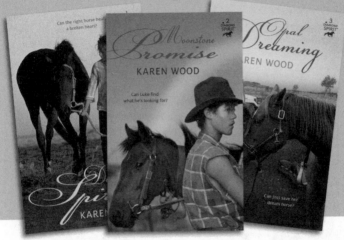

MOONSTONE PROMISE

Jess untied something from around her neck and held it out to Luke. 'Take my moonstone. They're supposed to give you beautiful dreams.'
It was a pale oval-shaped stone, hung on a thin leather strap.
'Promise me you'll come back,' she whispered.
'I'll see you again, Jess,' Luke said. 'Promise.'

After a harsh childhood spent in foster care, Luke finally feels at home on Harry's farm, working with horses. When Harry dies, and Luke has a bitter falling-out with the people around him, he does a runner, leaving everything behind. He takes off to the gulf country in search of brumbies and finds himself camped by a river with three Aboriginal elders.

Can a mob of wild brumbies and three wise men help Luke discover who he is and where he belongs?